* * * * *

To Maureen

my wife, closest companion and dearest friend

* * * * *

ALSO BY MICHAEL C. COX

* * * * *

NOVELS

Once Upon A Term

* * * * *

SHORT STORIES

Facts and Fantasies – Volume 1

Facts and Fantasies – Volume 3

Facts and Fantasies – Volume 4

Facts and Fantasies – Omnibus

* * * * *

Facts and Fantasies

Volume 2

Heart of Rotterdam

Michael C. Cox

Mimast Inc

Mimast Inc

This paperback edition published in 2015 by Mimast Inc

Copyright © Mimast Inc 2015,

Canadian ISBN 978-1-987926-01-9

All enquiries regarding this electronic edition to:

Mimast Inc
Edmonton
Alberta T6R 2H9
Canada
email: mimast@telus.net

Acknowledgements

Firstly, I must acknowledge a debt to the teachers who taught English language and English literature in my first five years at a Grammar school in my home town of Bristol. In spite of their efforts and best intentions, by the time I was sixteen I had acquired a taste for reading but not for writing. To be fair to those teachers, I felt at the time that I had so much to read and so little to write about.

I must acknowledge two of those teachers: Alex Mair, a Scotsman no less, and A.B. Reynolds, a somewhat eccentric Englishman. The former opened my eyes to literature by telling me to read Great Expectations by Charles Dickens. The latter opened my eyes to language by telling me to read out loud the first sentence in an exercise on syntax error: "Do not kill your wife with work, let electricity do it."

Secondly, I must thank my dear friend, Leif G. Stolee. He has encouraged me to write about people and events that have enriched my life over the past few decades. Leif's enthusiastic response to my stories has kept me at my computer and out of mischief. And I must mention here, James Stolee. He tempered his brother's enthusiasm with many well deserved criticisms of my writings.

Lastly but certainly not least, I must thank my wife, Maureen. She has always been my dearest and closest friend. She has watched over my grammar, corrected my spelling and made many constructive suggestions. Without Maureen's love and support, I doubt that I could ever have written a single word.

* * * * *

Needless to say, any mistakes in grammar and spelling, and any errors in facts used fictitiously, are my fault entirely. Nobody else is to blame.

* * * * *

THE FOUR STORIES

* * * * *

* * * * *

Author's note

The first of these stories is fiction inspired by some actual events related to me by some friends and acquaintances. Any resemblance of any character to anyone I knew is purely co-incidental. The second is a fond recollection of my father and relates actual events that still have me shaking my head and thinking, "What are the chances?" Behind the third story are real people and events. but the consequence of my crime is fictional albeit the logically expected result of a chemical reaction. The fourth of these four stories describes an actual incident involving real people I knew but whose actual names I have not disclosed. If by my descriptions I have unwittingly disclosed the identities of my former neighbours, I hope they will not be embarrassed or upset by my portrayal of them.

THE BEST LAID SCHEMES

My parents, like many people after World War II, did not have a car. I was fortunate. John, a friend of mine, taught me to drive his small Morris Oxford which he used for work. He was a travelling door-to-door brush salesman. John liked some of the people he met but disliked the job, so he eventually went back to work for an insurance company. He disliked that work rather less but some of his co-workers rather more. The idea for this story stems from my recollection of John's account of life as a salesman and an insurance clerk.

* * * * *

Sitting in his little car watching the sleet sliding down the windscreen, Alan White was wondering why he ever gave up his job with the Prudential Insurance Company. Their new building, on the corner of Wine Street in Bristol, opened in 1957 just a few months before he was taken on as a junior clerk. He would travel to the office by bus – a 15-minute ride – and be one of the first to sign in. His desk was in a corner next to a radiator. On a cold afternoon he could warm his outer coat before leaving the building. If his raincoat was wet when he arrived, it would be dry and warm when he left. The pay was good. With his Christmas bonus he could treat his father, Bill, to some pipe-tobacco and his mother, Ethel, to a bottle of port. So why did he quit?

* * * * *

Clerical work was dull. Little broke the daily routine. Now and then Eddie Warburton, the office comedian, might roar with laughter and read out loud from a claims form.

> *I thought my window was down but found it was up when I put my head through it.*

From time to time an attractive secretary-typist would pop in, smile and say hello as she dropped a new file on Alan's desk. On a rare occasion the senior clerk might put his head around the door and announce the opening of a new branch. This raised everybody's hopes of a change and a promotion but such hopes were short-lived. Anyway, Alan knew that even if he rose to the dizzy heights of senior clerk or assistant branch manager, he would still feel unfulfilled.

The tedious routine was a factor but only a minor one in his decision to quit. The major factor was that he fell foul of his co-workers. Alan was very serious-minded and could be rather shy. According to at least three long-serving clerks, he was also too honest for his own good. These three so-called colleagues came to their conclusion not long after Alan's mother was taken ill.

* * * * *

Rachel Wallace first met Rupert Coleman as she was leaving the Queens Road Branch of Lloyds Bank for her lunch break. He'd held the door open and stepped out in the sunshine with her. He said hello and disappeared. Later he re-appeared in the university refectory and asked if he might share her table. It never occurred to her that he wasn't a Bristol graduate or that their second encounter wasn't a coincidence. And it didn't strike her as particularly odd that he'd forgotten his wallet and let her pay for his coffee and sandwich lunch. As they stepped into University Road, he mentioned that he had two tickets for a piano recital at the Colston Hall that evening. 'Would she like to go?' She was flattered and she was free, so she said yes.

She waited for him that evening by the fountain in front of the Victoria Rooms. She had arrived a few minutes early. On the dot of six o'clock, he appeared from behind the fountain. 'Have I kept you waiting?' Before she could reply, he said, 'You look lovely.' Then he kissed her on the cheek. 'The recital starts at 7 o'clock so we've plenty of time. Do you mind walking?' Rachel, still blushing, said truthfully, 'No. I like walking.' They went along Queens Road into Park Row as far as the Christmas Steps. From there he held her hand as they walked down to Colston Street.

Denis Matthews began his recital with Mozart's Sonata in B Flat (K333) followed by Beethoven's Sonata in C Major Opus 53 (Waldstein). Rachel admired his formidable technique and prolific memory but found both works a little heavy going. In the interval over coffee, Rupert told her that the B Flat Sonata was one of a set of four that Mozart composed after his return to Salzburg from Paris in 1779. 'He may have written them for the mademoiselles Aloysia and Constanze Weber,' said Rupert, 'before he settled on marrying Constanze.'

Rachel liked the variety in the second half. She was not familiar with the six Bulgarian Dances by Bela Bartok but she knew Schumann's Kinderschenen – subtitled, according to the programme notes, *Scenes of Childhood from Strange Lands and Peoples*. When Denis Matthews was playing no.7 – Traümerei (Dreaming) and no.11 – *Fürchtenmachen* (Frightening), Rupert's long slender fingers seemed to be playing along on his knees.

As she listened to the three intermezzos and the rhapsody in E flat Op. 119/4 by Johannes Brahms, Rachel recalled the Dutchman, Johannes van Dijk, she'd met on the train to Southampton. He had sent her a picture postcard of Ossip Zadkine's statue - Stad Zonder Hart (city without heart) - from Rotterdam and promised to write her a letter.

She saw quite a bit of Rupert after that concert. They went out several times and he always walked her home. She allowed him to kiss her goodnight but absolutely refused to allow his hands to explore her body. Rachel was determined to be virgo intacto when she walked up the aisle to marry 'Mr. Right'. After her first rebuff, Rupert kept his hands to himself and seemed content with a goodnight kiss.

She enjoyed his company. He was charming, witty and fascinating when he talked about music. What she found less adorable was his readiness to borrow money and forget to pay her back. She was beginning to wonder how honest and trustworthy he was. And then one day his name cropped up during her investigations at Lloyds Bank.

'Open our hearts and minds, O Lord, to the knowledge and love of Thee. Amen.' intoned the Rev. George W. Stockport from the pulpit of the Baptist Church in East Street.

The evening sermon began like the morning service that Sunday. Alan preferred evensong and always looked forward to joining the minister and his wife at the Manse for tea, biscuits and discussions with other young people. The current theme for the Sunday sermons - and for the Wednesday evening Bible Study which Alan also always attended - was The Commandments. Alan preferred the alternative name The Decalogue which the Reverend Stockport had used at their first Bible Study on the topic. He liked the ring of the word which came from the Greek deka ten and logos word.

'My text is again taken from the Old Testament,' began the minister, 'and from the Book of Exodus, Chapter 20.' Alan opened his Bible – the King James Version. 'In the first four Commandments - *the religious commandments* - God describes our obligations to Him,' began the minister. 'First, we must worship no other god but Him. Second, we must not bow down and serve any graven image.' He paused, looked down at the congregation where a well-heeled banker was trying to keep his eyes open and said, 'Mammon – the false god of avarice.'

Alan remembered how, at Bible Study, they had distinguished between avarice and greed – two of the seven deadly sins. Greed for riches is avarice. Greed for food is gluttony. '*Third*,' continued the minister, 'we must not take the name of Our Lord in vain. *Fourth*, we must remember the Sabbath and keep it holy.' 'Amen,' murmured several worshippers.

'In the remaining six Commandments - *the ethical and moral commandments* - God describes our obligations to one another. So far we have considered four of these Commandments. We must honour our parents.' Alan thought the world of his mother, Ethel, who was at home ill in bed. 'We must not murder.' Alan didn't always see eye to eye with Bill and, after an argument, might well have said he'd like to strangle his dad but he never meant it. 'We must not commit adultery. We must not steal.'

'This evening,' said the Revered Stockport, 'we shall consider the fifth of these Commandments - Exodus Chapter 20 Verse 16 God's – *Thou shalt not bear false witness against thy neighbour.*' Alan's mind turned to his problem at work.

His dad, Bill, left the house at 4:30 every morning. This meant Alan had to get Ethel's breakfast, help her to eat it, make sure she took her medicine, help her to the bathroom and remake the bed before he tucked her back into it. Then he'd have to sprint down the road to catch the bus. Dr Pollard had confined her to bed on the Sunday afternoon. On the Monday morning Alan was almost the last to sign in. Only two people - Eddie Warburton and Jim Sparks - arrived at the office after him that day. On Tuesday, Wednesday and Thursday, Harry Davies also signed in after Alan.

The root of Alan's problem was his honesty. He always recorded his *actual* time of arrival. That first week it was around 9 a.m. The staff who arrived before him either put in false times or left their times blank. When Eddie, Jim and Harry arrived after Alan *and* after 9 o'clock, they *had* to record their times and *had* to show they were late. On the Friday of that first week, Alan arrived at 9:02. Eddie and Jim had arrived a few minutes before and put down 8:45 and 8:46. Harry arrived after Alan - well past 9 o'clock and late. When he saw Alan's time he exploded.

'What's wrong with you?' bellowed the elderly clerk. 'Why'd you have to put 9:02?

'That's when I signed in,' said Alan a little nervously.

'So? Now the boss will know we're late.'

'My mother's ill and...'

'The boss won't care,' snapped Harry. 'Now he knows we're late. That's it! You, you ...'

'I'll tell him my mum's ill. He'll understand.'

'And what'll I tell the boss?' growled Harry.

'It's not my fault you're late' said Alan, going slightly hot under the collar.

What's wrong with you, lad? You just don't get it, do you. We cover for one another here. You scratch our backs and we'll scratch yours.'

'By telling lies! Sorry, I cannot bear false witness.'

'You cannot bear false witness! Who do you think you are, you sanctimonious little twit,' Harry fumed and stormed off.

It was several more weeks before Alan's mother got better and he could catch his early bus again. During those weeks the atmosphere in the office deteriorated. He felt isolated. Even that attractive secretary-typist stopped smiling and saying hello when she brought him a file. Finally, Alan gave in his notice. He cleared out his desk and left the building for the last time on a Friday afternoon.

On the Sunday evening after church he told the Reverend Stockport what had happened. The minister was sympathetic and asked Alan what he planned to do now. 'I thought I might apply to the Bristol Baptist College to study theology and become a minister,' said Alan, 'What do you think?' George Stockport thought carefully and said, 'If you can stay out, then you should stay out. Only enter the ministry if you really must.'

When Alan told his mum and dad that he'd given up his job with the Prudential and was thinking of studying to be a Baptist minister, Ethel said, 'I think you'd make a lovely vicar, dear.' Before he could explain that the Anglican Church had vicars, the Baptist Church had ministers and the Roman Catholic Church had priests, Bill said, 'That was a cushy job you had at the Pru'. What'll you do for money now? Vicars don't earn much, do they?'

Alan grinned. Thinking of Eddie back in the office, he said, 'I heard three boys arguing about whose dad earned most. The postman's son said his father worked six days a week and earned £600 a year. The bank manager's son said his father worked five

13

days and earned £1200 a year. The third boy, a vicar's son, said, 'I don't know how much mine earns but he only works one day a week and it takes six men to carry his wages up to him.' Bill laughed.

Ethel didn't get the joke. 'It's not funny,' she said, turning to Alan. 'Perhaps you could get a job at the Central Telephone Exchange, dear. You know, at the Bristol Exchange where the Queen and the Duke of Edinburgh were last December.' Alan explained that Bristol had been chosen for the first ever Subscriber Trunk Dialling exchange and the Queen came on the 5th of December 1958 to make the first ever S.T.D. call. 'Her Majesty called the Lord Provost of Edinburgh, 365 miles away. An electronic robot called Grace connected Her call. I don't think they'd want me now they've got Grace,' said Alan, opening the Bristol Evening Post to the situations vacant column.

WANTED
KLEENEZE SALES AGENTS
Apply NOW

* * * * *

The sleet was still sliding down the windscreen and showing little sign of stopping. Alan had dropped his two passengers at the front entrance before driving to the car park behind the building. The two of them would be in their seats and waiting for him. The thought of having to make a dash for the door reminded him of his time as a Kleeneze salesman and he began to wonder why he quit that job.

* * * * *

He sold brushes and other products door-to-door for Kleeneze but he was actually self-employed. He was his own boss and answered only to himself. When his dad became ill, he took time off to visit him in hospital. Alan himself had always been fit and healthy. At school he'd played rugby and soccer for the first teams. During his two years of National Service in the Royal Air Force he played soccer for the squadron. He also learned ballroom dancing in the RAF. When he was demobbed, he took up badminton and tennis.

Whatever the weather, he enjoyed being outdoors. He usually had a healthy-looking tan to go with his dark hair, brown eyes and white teeth. Alan's customers referred to him as Mr Kleeneze or Smiler. They liked him. He liked them. For a short while he was earning good money - more than he was getting at the Pru and far more than he was getting now. So why did he quit?

Kleeneze wasn't the problem. It was a good company founded in Bristol in 1923 by one Harry Crook who was anything but crooked. Alan knew him to be honest, hardworking and genuinely concerned for his workers, sales force and the community. In 1938 he founded the Bristol 5 Boys Club – a Youth Activities and Education Centre – at his company premises in Chalk Road, Bristol 5. In 1959 Harry Crook he was the first in Britain to introduce the 40-hour working week in his factory. He served the City of Bristol as an Alderman, Sheriff and eventually Lord Mayor.

Alan knew Dr Crook's background: senior executive for the Fuller Company in America; returned to Britain in 1920; started a brush-twisted-in-wire business with a workbench in rented factory space; modelled himself on Alfred Carl Fuller. Alan didn't know that Fuller was a farm boy from Nova Scotia, Canada, who started his business with a small workshop in his sister's basement in Somerville near Boston, Massachusetts. Harry and Alfred were both determined to make the best brushes and sell them by direct marketing.

Harry Crook ran Kleeneze like a family business. He'd tour his factory every morning and talk with individual workers. He published a weekly bulletin, called Searchlight, to keep the salesmen informed of company progress. Alan always read it hoping to find hints and tips to improve his sales technique. Harry gave his door-to-door salesmen a 40% commission on the price of every item they sold. The more they sold the more they earned. This appealed to Alan who had never been afraid of hard work.

Harry's brother, George Crook, was responsible for sales. At his regular meetings he'd hand out song sheets and lead the salesmen in a sing-song to boost their morale. Alan had a good voice and liked singing, so he would join in but he didn't think much of the

Kleeneze songs. He preferred the traditional hymns they sang at East Street Baptist Church.

At George Crook's meetings Alan often overheard old hands telling stories and offering advice.

'Watch out for dogs – they can be trouble. Keep your suitcase between them and your legs. Walk up the path like you're a friend of the family. If a dog goes for you, don't kick it. If you do, the owner's bound to see you and bang goes a customer.'

'What if he bites you?'

'You mean the dog not the customer, right?' They all laughed.

'Put on a brave face. Smile. Praise the owner for having a good guard dog. Ask the owner for a sticking plaster to put on the bite. You'll probably get a bit of sympathy. It worked for me once. The lady of the house asked me in, put the plaster on my leg and after my demo she ordered three brushes and two tins of lavender polish. Now every time I go back there she always asks after my leg.'

Alan was a bit discouraged when he heard salesmen bragging about their sales. One old hand said, 'I get through four 50-page order books every week.'

'Four books! Crikey! That's a lot. How many deliveries do you make?'

'About 200 each week.'

Alan didn't fill one book in his first month.

'Anybody ever cancel when you deliver?'

'Quite often – usually when the husband's home.'

'What do you do then?'

'Depends. Usually I ask them which brush they can manage without till my next visit.'

'That's my trick,' said another old hand from Lancashire. 'It works well does that.'

That last comment made Alan uncomfortable. When he became a salesman he'd refused to believe his job was to persuade people to buy something they didn't need and probably wouldn't use with money they couldn't afford. He didn't want to *trick* people. He wanted to earn an honest living. So far he hadn't been bitten by a dog and he hadn't tricked anybody but then he hadn't had many orders or made many deliveries. In short, he wasn't doing very well. One day all this changed.

* * * * *

Rupert had hardly been able to believe his eyes when Kate produced the tickets for the two-day weekend trip to Amsterdam. 'Happy Birthday,' she said, giving him a big kiss. What a girl and what a treat. They had flown into Schipol, Amsterdam's International Airport - eleven feet below sea level according to the brochure – and taken a taxi to the Hotel Zandberg where they booked in as Mr. & Mrs. Spencer. After unpacking their overnight bags and testing the resilience of the bed springs, they dined in a small restaurant close to the Concertgebouw.

They enjoyed the concert, especially Mozart's Symphony No. 40 in G Minor – known as the 'Great' – 'to distinguish it,' Rupert said, 'from Wolfgang's No. 25, the only other minor symphony he wrote.' Kate was sorry not to have heard Amsterdam's Concertgebouw Orchestra conducted by Bernard Haitink but thought the Rotterdam Philharmonic played very well.

The hotel bed springs were severely tested again before they turned out the light and went to sleep. After a late breakfast the following morning, they followed the advice of the concierge and took a sight-seeing trip around the canals of Amsterdam - the Venice of the North according to the advertisement - before taking a taxi back to Schipol and their plane to London Heathrow. On the return flight, it struck Rupert just how different Kate and Rachel were from one another.

* * * * *

The letter bearing a Dutch stamp and a Rotterdam postmark arrived in the morning before Rachel left for the office. She put it in her briefcase and hurried to catch the bus to Prince Street. She kept the letter to open and read it over lunch in the canteen.

Antiek, Kunst, Juwelen, Boeken en Horloges
Johannes van Dijk

Dear Rachel,

I hope that you liked my postcard to show you the statue of Zadkine. As I told you already, he made it to remember us of the bombing and destroying of the Rotterdam Centrum.

My son – Pieter – and I should like very much to show you something of Holland. So we invite you to come for a few days to stay with us. If you would take the train to Harwich and then the night boat from there we shall meet you at Hoek van Holland and bring you by auto to Rotterdam.

Please. Write me when can you come.

Greetings from

Johannes van Dijk

Rachel had been seeing Rupert – irregularly rather than regularly - for a while but with no commitment on either side. She *had* enjoyed the Dutchman's company on that train journey from Bristol to Southampton and saw nothing sinister in his invitation. And she definitely needed a break. So, that afternoon she asked her head of department for some leave and in the evening she wrote to Johannes. On the Saturday when she received a reply from Johannes, she booked her train and night ferry return ticket.

On the following Thursday she took her overnight suitcase to the office and left work promptly after lunch, taking a taxi to Temple Meads Station. At Paddington Station she took the underground to Victoria Station for the train to Harwich. She was on the deck of the S.S. Arnhem when it sailed at 10:15 p.m. The North Sea crossing was smooth and the bed comfortable but she didn't sleep very well. The cabin was rather stuffy. And, she admitted to herself, she was excited at the prospect of seeing Johannes again. The ship docked at the Hook of Holland 6:15 a.m. local time.

Friday

As she disembarked, she saw Johannes and Pieter – tall and fair-haired just like his father – smiling and waving from the quay. 'How are you Johannes,' she said as they shook hands. 'Jan. Remember I told you already to call me Jan. This is my son Pieter.' He shook her hand. 'Piet. You must call me by that name, ja,' he said. 'Please, I take your case.'

Rachel thought Piet was going to drive but then realised that the steering wheel was on the left. 'Please,' said Piet, opening the front passenger door of the pale grey Alfa Romeo grey sedan, 'you sit here.' When she was settled comfortably on the white, soft leather bench seat, he closed her door and climbed into the back with her suitcase.

'Your journey was good?'

'Yes, very good, thank you Jan,' she said. 'Is it far to your house?'

'Not far at all. I suppose about 27 kilometres – I should better say 17 miles. Actually we live in Schiedam – a suburb a few kilometres south west of Rotterdam Centrum.'

Seeing the signs for Maasdijk and Maassluis, Piet leant forward and said, 'De Maas is what you call The Meuse. It is a major river from France that comes through Belgium then Holland before it goes into the North Sea. Altogether 925 kilometres.'

'd-i-j-k means dike, I assume,' said Rachel, 'but what is s-l-u-i-s?'

'Ja,' said Piet, 'it means a *sluice* or you can better say *lock* to control water levels.'

'Oh, look, a windmill – and its sails are turning!'

'Ja, that is De Wippersmolen here in Maassluis. It's a drainage or polder mill. We call him a *draai kop molen*.'

'I know a polder is low lying land reclaimed from the sea. But,' asked Rachel, trying her best to say the name properly, 'what's a *dry cop mowlan*?'

'I may say *turn head mill* because we can turn him at the top for the wind to come at the sails. During the occupation the resistance used the windmills to send signals. The Germans didn't know we do that, niet waar, Vader?'

Johannes said, 'Ja, that's true. We could fix the sails into different positions, like + or x, and send coded messages from mill to mill.'

'Were you in the Dutch Resistance, Jan?'

'Ja, we both were,' said Piet proudly, 'even when I was only seven years.'

'You were very brave, Piet. Moeder was proud of you,' said Johannes.

'Zo, thuis,' said Piet as the car pulled up outside their house, on the corner of the Arij Prinslaan, just opposite the Julianapark.

Piet led the way carrying her suitcase. Rachel followed. Jan locked the car and caught them up. Before they reached the house, the front door opened and a young woman rushed out. She kissed Piet and said, 'Zo, hebben jullie honger. Ik heb 't ontbijt klaar. Oh, sorry, you must be Rachel, yes? May I just introduce myself. My name is Lies. I am Piet's verloofde – fianceé. You have hunger? I have breakfast ready. Please. Come in.'

On the table there were Edam and Gouda cheeses, a plate covered with thin slices of smoked meat (*rookvlees*), a bowl of hard-boiled eggs still in their shells, dishes of jam - strawberry and black currant, a basket with slices of three different kinds of bread and a dish of butter. There was a coffee pot and also what looked like an oversized purse containing a large tea pot. When they were all seated, Jan said quietly, 'In de naam van de Vader, en de Zoon, en de Heilige Geest. Amen.' Piet offered the basket of bread to Rachel and said, 'Eet smakelijk.' Jan said, 'It's how we say *bon appétit* in Dutch.'

Immediately after breakfast, Jan showed her around the house and garden while Piet helped Elise clear the table and wash the dishes. Then Jan drove them all into Rotterdam. There were so many bridges, big and small, over so many waterways. When Rachel asked, Piet confessed that even he could not always tell the differences between *kanaal*, *gracht*, *singel* and *sloot*. 'I believe,' he said, 'that *singel* comes out of Latin *cingulum* – girdle because in the beginning it was usually a moat around the city.'

When they approached the Belasting & Douane Museum, Rachel told Jan politely that she was on holiday and didn't want to think about taxes & customs. Jan and Piet laughed. Elise told Rachel they were not serious about going in there although the museum was interesting. It was the Prins Hendrik Nautical Museum they visited first before they took a luxury boat tour, run by Spido, around Rotterdam harbour – the largest harbour in Europe.

In the afternoon, after what, in Rachel's opinion, they mistakenly described as a *light lunch*, they went shopping in the Lijnbaan. This pedestrian precinct and shopping centre – the first of its kind in Europe – was opened in 1953. Jan took her to his shop where he showed her an antique Delft Blue & White brooch, 1 inch in diameter and domed, depicting a windmill scene. The ceramic was surrounded by 25 tiny intricate florets in 835 Sterling silver. The brooch was authentically signed on the back.

'Do you like this?' Jan asked. 'Zo, let me pin it on your lapel.' In a moment his large hands had expertly worked the antique T-bar hinge and wire clasp. 'What do you think?'

With a smile at Piet, Rachel said, 'It's a draai kop molen, isn't it.'

Piet smiled. 'Ja. Zeker,' he said.

'Dat is zo fraai – sorry, beautiful!' said Elise clapping her hands together.

When Rachel went to unpin the brooch Jan took hold of her arm and said, 'Please, keep it on. It is a souvenir from me for your visit to Holland.'

On the way back to Schiedam, Jan drove through Delfshaven - the oldest part of Rotterdam – to the Aelbrechtskolk and the historic church where the Pilgrim Fathers held their last service before embarking on the *Speedwell*. Piet explained that a *kolk* is the section of water between two sets of lock gates. 'It buffers between the high and low water,' said Piet.

Rachel said to Jan, 'I always thought the Pilgrim Fathers sailed in the Mayflower from Plymouth.'

Jan smiled and said, 'Ja, that is so but those people started with two ships first from Southampton. Then bad weather drove them into Plymouth Sound where they abandoned the Speedwell because it was a leaky old tub. That's what you do, ja, when something is no good for you.' She would recall his words later when she was back in England.

In the evening, after they had eaten another substantial meal, they sat in comfortable chairs and Jan poured them all a small glass of *jenever*, a traditional Dutch liqueur made from juniper berries. It was strongly alcoholic. Even a small sip burned the back of Rachel's throat. In Holland people generally did not close their curtains when it got dark. So, anyone walking by the house could look in to see the potted plants lining the window sill and the people sitting in the room drinking jenever.

'It is good that you visit Holland now,' said Jan, 'because tomorrow we have the opportunity to hear the Rotterdamse Philharmonisch Orkest conducted by Eduard Flipse in the Concertgebouw in Amsterdam.' The Rotterdam concert building was destroyed by the Luftwaffe in 1940.

Piet explained that Eduard Flipse was raising money to build a new hall for the RPhO on Schouwburgplein. 'Vader is helping with that,' he said proudly.

When she saw Rachel stifle a yawn, Elise said, 'Moe – tired? Rachel nodded. 'So, please, you should go to bed. Tomorrow we go to Amsterdam.' They all stood up and Elise said, 'Goeje nacht. Welterusten. Sorry – goodnight. Sleep well.'

Saturday

Rachel, Jan and Piet had an early breakfast on Saturday morning. Rachel helped Piet to clear the table and wash up. Jan disappeared into his study. As soon as Elise arrived, all four piled into the car for Amsterdam. Piet was a mine of information. 'I should tell you,' he said, 'that the capital of Noord Holland is Haarlem and of Zuid Holland is Amsterdam – Den Haag (The Hague) is the seat of our government. It doesn't matter to me. I prefer Amsterdam. It has 1,281 bridges and 165 canals. Many people live on the water in houseboats.' Elise told Rachel she would not want to do that and said, 'You will see such places in some moments because we are going to tour the canals with the rondvaart.'

Jan parked near the railway station and they walked across the road to the Hendrik Kade for the rondvaart (round sailing) in a long, glass-topped boat. Their guide – a student from Amsterdam university – gave the commentary enthusiastically first in Dutch, English, French and Spanish – always in that order. Often she described, in the first four languages, what to look for.

'Ladies and Gentleman, in a moment by the canal on your right you may see a bird cage outside a window of the house of Rembrandt where he worked from 1639 till 1658.' By the time she said this unenthusiastically in the fifth language, German, the boat would have gone past the canal and the bird cage. At the end of the tour the guide said in a matter-of-fact way, 'Thank you for your kind attention. I hope you enjoyed your trip. Please be aware that you are permitted to grant gratuities to the guide.' As they disembarked Rachel gave her a tip and a big thank you.

'Koffie, jongens?' said Jan indicating a table outside a café. 'Alsjeblieft,' said Piet, 'met slagroom.' Elise translated, 'Coffee, youngsters. Please – with whipped cream.' Rachel resolved to diet when she got home. After coffee they walked up the Dam Rak to the Royal Palace. Jan said, 'Buckingham Palace has more grandeur, ja?' Rachel had to agree. They took a tram to the Rijksmuseum to see Rembrandt's famous Nightwatch painting. Around lunchtime, they went on a tram back to the station for the car. Jan drove them to the Vondelpark to eat the picnic lunch Elise had prepared.

After lunch they strolled around the park – Amsterdam's largest – which was designed as an English landscape by the architect L. D. Zocher in 1864 and opened in 1865. Jan showed Rachel the statue of the most famous Dutch poet Joost van der Vondel. 'He lived from 1587 to 1679,' said Jan, 'and converted to Roman Catholicism in 1641. Many of his poems were inspired by his conversion and by his grief at the death of his wife as well as three of his five children.' Rachel wondered how Jan's wife had died.

They walked from the park to the Stedelijkmuseum to see one of van Gogh's famous Sunflower paintings. 'Look,' said Jan, 'this has fifteen sunflowers in the vase. Vincent painted them in 1889 in Arles. Altogether there are seven paintings with a vase – three with 15 flowers, two with 12, one with 5 and one with 3 flowers. All seven were painted in Arles between August 1888 and January 1889. The sunflowers he painted in Paris in 1887 are not in a vase; we call them cut flowers.'

After another so-called light meal at a Dutch-Indonesian restaurant they headed to the Concertgebouw. The Rotterdam Philharmonic Orchestra's performances of Ludvig von Beethoven's Egmont Ouverture and his Fifth Symphony were superb. The applause was long and loud. 'Odd,' thought Rachel, 'how the Dutch still dislike the Germans but like their music.'

During the interval, when Piet was telling Rachel how the first four notes of the 5th symphony matched the Morse code for Sir Winston Churchill's 'V' for victory, he saw a sudden look of surprise on her face. 'You didn't know this?'

She looked back at Piet and said, 'Sorry, Piet, what did you say?'

Jan was concerned. He'd seen her startled look. 'Are you alright?'

As she replied, 'Oh, yes, thank you Jan. I thought I saw ...' a bell warned people to return to their seats.

When they were leaving the hall at the end of the concert, Rachel seemed to Jan to be looking for someone. As he drove past along the Oude Groenmarkt, he heard Rachel gasp and out of the corner of his eye he saw her put her hand over her mouth. 'Have you left something behind,' he asked her, 'because I can turn back.' Rachel didn't hear him. Her head was spinning. Rupert, with his arm around a dark curly-haired young woman, was going into a hotel. 'So it was him I saw at the concert,' she said to herself.

Sunday

Elise joined them for Rachel's third Dutch breakfast. Afterwards Jan helped her to clear the table and wash up so that Piet could tell Rachel how Dutch Hydraulic Engineers had turned a saltwater sea (De Zuider Zee) into a freshwater lake (Het Ijsselmeer).

'From Noord Holland to Friesland we built a dijk 32 km long, 90 m wide and 7.25 m above the sea level. It took us from 1927 to 1932. We began the building from four positions – from two on the mainlands and from two artificial islands we made on the line of the dijk. The Afsluitdijk (off-shut-dike) was opened officially 25 September 1933. Of course,' said Piet, 'the Germans bombed holes into it in the war.'

Piet was just about to show Rachel technical cross-section diagrams of the dike when Jan put his head around the door and said, 'Hou op, jongen. Wij zijn klaar.' Piet smiled and told Rachel his father had just said, 'Shut up, young man. We are ready.'

It was a whirlwind tour. Rotterdam to Delft where Rachel's antique brooch originated. On to Den Haag – the seat of the

Government. From the Hague to Leiden. 'We could spend a week here,' said Jan, 'and still not see everything. Rembrandt – full name Rembrandt Harmenszoon van Rijn was born in Leiden on the 15th July 1606. He was the eighth of nine children from Harmen Gerritszoon van Rijn and his wife Neeltje (little Nell or Nellie). Zoon means son. So Rembrandt was Harmen's son.'

Rachel nodded and said, 'So Rembrandt's grandfather was called Gerrit.'

Jan patted her on the back and said, 'Een knap meisje.'

Elise whispered in Rachel's ear, 'Intelligent girl.'

After coffee they drove slowly through Haarlem, the Capital of Nord Holland, without stopping. 'We shall go through Alkmaar,' said Jan, 'but the kaasmarkt - cheese market - is only for Fridays, so we cannot see men in fancy dress running about carrying those cheeses.'

When they reached the south end of the Afsluitdijk, Rachel was stunned to see the road ahead stretching out across the water. With the North Sea on their left and the Ijssel Lake on their right, Jan drove the five miles to the monument - designed by the architect W.M. Dudok. 'This is the place,' said Piet, 'where, at 2 minutes over 1 o'clock on the 28th May 1932, we finally closed the dijk to keep out the sea.'

They ate their picnic lunch there but inside the car because outside the wind was quite cold. 'We can better call the Afsluitdijk a barrier dam,' said Piet. 'It has twenty-five discharge sluices and a shipping lock at each end to control the water levels.' Rachel could see why they needed locks but not why they needed the sluices. 'Ja,' said Piet, 'because the Ijssel river all the time puts water into the lake. We cannot let the Ijsselmeer fill up and overflow.'

The journey back to Schiedam seemed quite short. Rachel remarked on the flatness of the land with so much of it divided into so many neat, orderly farms. Shortly after they passed a signpost for Hoorn, Piet said to Rachel, 'Now I think you must know that water there on our left.' When she said the Ijssel lake, she heard Jan say, 'Ja, een knap meisje.'

They stopped in Edam for coffee. Only Rachel refused the whipped cream. 'The cheese market is here Wednesdays,' said Lies, ' so we don't see it. Anyway it's mostly a show for the tourists. In a moment we shall be in Volendam. There may be some people in traditional costumes – white high-pointed bonnets, fancy bodice with full, black skirts hiding their wooden clogs – what you see on postcards. More nonsense for the tourists.'

At Volendam Jan found a little car park and they walked through the cobbled streets to the edge of the Ijsselmeer to look at the colourful, quaint wooden houses. Rachel actually saw a few elderly woman in rather drab costumes. Their gnarled hands and wrinkled faces spoke of their long lives as fishermen's wives. They seemed care-worn and oblivious of Rachel. 'They have a simple, hard life here,' said Jan. 'Let's go home.'

Before the evening meal that Elise was preparing, Rachel first packed her suitcase then looked into the kitchen. 'Can I help?' Rachel asked Lies. 'No, thank you,' said Lies, 'I shall call you in about ten minutes.' Piet was reading in a chair by the window.

Rachel knocked on the study door. 'Binnen,' said Jan. Guessing that meant come in, she went in. Jan was sitting behind his desk. He stood up. 'Please, come in.' He was holding a framed photograph in his hand.

'This was my wife.'

'When did she die?'

'I don't know exactly,' said Jan. 'The Gestapo took her and her parents away when Piet and I were not at home.' His face hardened. 'A quisling neighbour told the Germans she and her mother were Joden – Jews. It was not true but those animals took them anyway. Piet never saw his mother again.' Then he looked at the photograph and sighed. 'One day I may be able to forgive but I never forget what those Nazis did to us.' The look on Jan's face was the same one that Rachel saw when they stood together in front of Zadkine's statue – city without a heart. Just as she reached out to touch Jan's arm, she heard Elise call out, 'Eten.'

When Johannes drove Rachel back to the Hoek van Holland on Monday to catch the 11:40 p.m. night boat back to Harwich, Piet and Elise came as well to see her off. All three stood under a light on the quay so she would see them smiling and waving goodbye. They had made her so welcome. She had eaten more in those three days than she normally ate in a week. As she curled up in the cabin bed she tried to think about all the places they had seen and all the things they done. Just as she was drifting off to sleep, a picture came into her mind of Rupert and a young woman entering the Hotel Zandberg.

* * * * *

Still sitting in his car, Alan remembered his first chance meeting with Rupert. As he watched a piece of ice slither down the car windscreen, he thought, 'Slippery and sliding on a downward path to disappear when it reaches the bottom. Yes, just like Rupert.'

* * * * *

He was pretty fed up. The week had been an utter disaster. Friday already and what had he to show for his efforts. Three small orders and one pair of sore feet. Long Ashton had been a dead loss. The only thing good about the place was the Angel Inn. He decided to cheer himself up with a half of cider and a Cornish pasty for lunch. He took his food and drink from the bar and sat at a small table by a window. As usual he was feeling hard done by. He'd had no choice but to resign from his first job. Now here he was trying to sell brushes door to door. How utterly ghastly. Just as he took a sip of his cider, he heard, 'Excuse me. May I join you?'

'Suit yourself,' he said without looking up. Alan put his orange juice and ham sandwich on the table and sat down. He picked up his sandwich from the plate, looked across the table and frowned. The sandy-coloured hair, blue eyes, long nose, thin lips and dimpled chin reminded him of someone from the past – his time in the RAF perhaps. Rupert sensed Alan's stare and looked up. 'Crikey!

28

Chalky? Chalky White?' Suddenly Alan grinned and said, 'Mustard? Well I'm blowed! Fancy meeting you here.'

'It's been a long time since anyone called me Mustard,' said Rupert, whose full name was Nicholas Rupert Spencer Coleman. 'Coleman's mustard,' he mused, 'I wonder if there's a Monsieur de Dijon in France with the nickname Moutarde.'

Alan grinned. 'Nobody's called me Chalky since I left school.' Reaching across to shake hands, he said, 'It's Alan, by the way. And you are ...?'

'Rupert but I sometimes answer to Ru. Anything but Nicholas or Old Nick.'

'What did you do when you left the Sixth Form?' asked Alan. 'University?'

'No. I tried for Maths and Physics at Bristol but didn't get a place. So I had to do National Service. What about you?'

'Straight from school into the RAF for two years. After that I got a job with the Prudential.'

'I went into the RAF as well. Signed on for three years. Got more pay and became a Personnel Selection Assessor. Absolute farce. When I finished training they sent me to the transit camp at Felixstowe. Second day there, I'm in the canteen playing the piano and the camp's commander walks in. What's your name corporal?' he says to me.

'Coleman, Sir!

"Carry on, corporal," he says and stands there listening.'

'Then what?' said Alan.

'Well, the next thing I know, he asks me to play Cole Porter's Begin the Beguine. When I finish, he says to me, "Staff dance on Saturday – 19 hundred hours sharp. Band needs a pianist." and marches off.

Alan remembered how well Rupert played the school piano for assembly and asked, 'What was that tune you used to play as we marched out of the school hall in the mornings?'

'Crikey! Mendelssohn's War March of the Priests. I haven't played that since school,' said Rupert humming the first few bars in his head.

'Anyway,' continued Rupert, 'instead of one week *in transit* I was there for nearly a year as the camp's pianist. Then we got a new commander - tone deaf! So, yours truly, Corporal Coleman, Sir, was posted to an RAF station in the middle of the Abu Dhabi desert. Half dozen tents, a million sand flies and no piano. The crazy thing was they already had a Personnel Selection Assessor – a sergeant! Two of us in the middle of the desert and nobody to assess. Actually, we did have forms from two servicemen to look at. One said he wanted to be a *gonner*. "He'll be a gonner when I get my hands on 'im" said serge. The other wanted to a *laft bincher*. We never saw him to interview so we never found out what a laft bincher was.'

'What did you do when you were demobbed?' asked Alan.

'Banking,' said Rupert. 'Lloyds Bank – the branch in Queens Road.'

'I know,' said Alan. 'next to the University. Popular with students I expect.'

'Yes,' said Rupert. 'that's how I met Rachel.'

'Your wife?'

'A girl friend. We *might* get engaged one day *if* I can afford a ring.'

'Is she a student?'

'She was. Got an economics degree at Bristol and works for the Inland Revenue now, so I suppose I've got to watch my step. What about you? A big noise in the Pru'?'

'No. It didn't suit me. I left. Now I'm a sales agent for Kleeneze,' said Alan diffidently.

'I don't believe it. A door-to-door brush salesman,' exclaimed Rupert.

'What's wrong with that?' asked Alan with a frown.

'Absolutely nothing at all, old boy,' said Rupert. 'Guess what I'm doing now.'

'Branch Manager at Lloyds in Queens Road?'

'No such luck,' said Rupert. 'No, I'm a sales agent for Betterware.'

'Not Betterware brushes?' said Alan. 'Well I'm blowed.'

* * * * *

Before she left her office for a lunch break, Rachel put the file – *Confidential/Investigate: Lloyds Bank, Queens Road Branch* – into her metal cabinet and locked the drawer. She waved to Ron, the security officer behind the front desk, as she headed for the front door of the Inland Revenue building in Prince Street. 'Out for a bit of sunshine, miss?' She looked at him with her green eyes, smiled and with a nod of her head stepped out into the street.

The sun was bright so she put on her sunglasses and turned right into Prince Street. Two engineers working on an overhead telephone line gave her wolf whistles. As she passed below their perch they looked down to see her straight fair hair held back by two brown tortoiseshell clips. As she walked away towards the city centre, they admired her slender figure dressed in a tailored dark olive jacket and skirt and whistled again. She barely noticed. She was out in the fresh air to think.

For her favourite walk, Rachel was wearing soft brown leather shoes with sensible flat heels. From Prince Street she went along Broad Quay into Colston Avenue where she paused to look at Edmund Burke – actually at his bronze statue cast in 1894 and the work of James Harvard Thomas. The replica in Washington DC was erected in 1922. She recalled that Burke - a distinguished philosopher – had been a controversial MP for Bristol from 1774 to 1780. She read the engraving on the plinth:

I wish to be a member of parliament to have my share of doing good and resisting evil

With those words going around in her head, Rachel turned into St Stephens Street and headed to Corn Street where she stopped to look at the four Nails – round-topped pedestals - outside the Exchange. Merchants and traders used to place their money on those pedestals when they struck a bargain. They called it *paying on the nail*. She tried not to think about the money Rupert owed her.

She retraced her steps through St Leonards Archway, crossed St Stephens Street into Clare Street and took the shortest route back to her office. Ron the security officer was still behind his desk. 'Good afternoon Miss Wallace. There was a telephone call for you,' he said, handing her a note. 'Mr Coleman.' Her heart missed a beat. 'Thank you, Ron,' she said.

* * * * *

'How long have you been with Kleeneze?' asked Rupert.

'Not long. A few months but it seems longer.'

'Same here. How's it going?' asked Rupert. Then before Alan could reply, he said, 'I've had a terrible week – month actually. This door-to-door sales lark isn't the money spinner I need.' He pulled a face at the thought of his debts.

'I've taken a few orders this week,' said Alan. 'Bit better than usual but nothing to shout about.'

'You shouldn't have any trouble. Kleeneze stuff is good - better than Betterware.'

'I thought Betterware's stuff was better – like the name suggests. If I wasn't a Kleeneze agent, I'd recommend Betterware brushes.'

A strange look came over Rupert's face. 'I've just remembered what someone said to me - Praise from your enemy is worth more than praise from your friend - and it's given me an idea.'

'Sorry? What are you getting at?' asked Alan.

'Look here. Suppose I tell people that Kleeneze brushes are better than mine – better quality and better value. Then a couple of days later you show them your brushes. I'll bet you a pound to a penny you'd get an order on the spot.'

'But your brushes are better than mine,' said Alan.

'Who cares?' said Rupert.

'But only one can be better. They can't both be better than the other.'

'Look, it doesn't matter. Here's the plan. First part of the week I'll tell people Kleeneze stuff is better than mine. You tell people Betterware stuff is better than yours. Second part of the week ...'

Alan interrupted him and, with a frown, said 'Wouldn't we be bearing false witness?'

'False witness? What *are* you on about? Look, I think your Kleeneze stuff is better than mine, right? You think my Betterware stuff is better than yours, right? So, who's telling lies? Where was I? Oh, yes, Second part of the week, I'll sell my stuff to your people and you sell your stuff to my people.'

'Will it work?'

'It's bound to. We'll clean up.' said Rupert. Then seeing Alan's doubtful look, he said, 'I'll tell you what - let's try it out. I'll do a house this afternoon and meet you back here at 3 o'clock. Then you go there and make your pitch. What d'you say?'

* * * * *

Rachel sat down and read Rupert's note. At quarter past two the phone on her desk rang. 'Rachel Wallace.'

'Rachel – this is Rupert. How are you?'

'Bit busy actually. Something wrong? You don't normally call me at my office.'

'No, nothing wrong. I just need your help.'

Her heart missed beat. Hoping it wasn't money again, she asked, 'What do you want?'.

'Could you be home with your parents by four o'clock this afternoon?' He then explained what he wanted her to do and, in his usual smooth way, talked her into doing it. Rupert could always turn on the charm.

* * * * *

At ten past four that Friday afternoon, Alan walked up the garden path and rang the doorbell of number 48 Pembroke Road, Clifton, Bristol 8. Doris saw him and called out to her daughter, 'Rose, there's a young man coming up the path. He's carrying a suitcase. Would you answer the door. He looks a nice young man.' As Rose went to the door she said, 'Looks can be very deceptive, mother.' Doris sighed. 'I know dear.'

The young woman took his breath away. 'Um, er, good afternoon, um, miss, er, madam,' Alan mumbled. Then taking hold of himself, he started again. 'Good afternoon. I'm your local representative.'

She smiled and asked, 'Conservative, Labour or Liberal?'

'Oh, sorry. I'm not ... No, sorry. Excuse me. I'm your local Kleeneze agent. If it's convenient I should like five minutes to show what we have to make life easier for you around the house. May I come in?'

'Kleeneze you say?'

'Yes.'

'I think we can spare five minutes. Come in.'

She showed him into the living room. Alfred was sitting bolt upright in his wing-back chair near the fireplace with his back to the window - shoulders back like a soldier on parade. His strong hands gripped the arms of the chair and his shiny black shoes were planted firmly together on the rug in front of him. Doris was sitting more comfortably on the two-seater settee on the other side of the fireplace. Rose went and sat down by her mother. They all turned and looked at Alan. He put his case on the rug and knelt down facing the fire.

Nervously, he opened his case and began his demonstration. He didn't falter until he showed them the lavender polish tin. Holding out her delicate hand, Rose said, 'May I see that?' He handed her the tin. She tried to open it by twisting the little lever on the side. 'Let me,' said Alan.

He was all fingers and thumbs. Suddenly the lid flew off and landed on Rose's shoe. 'Oh, I'm so sorry,' he said. Doris was smiling at him. Rose laughed and said, 'No harm done. My shoes could do with a polish anyway.'

Alan, somewhat red in the face, said, 'Actually it's furniture polish. It really does make wood shine.'

'Time for a nice cup of tea,' said Doris, easing her plump figure out of the settee and smoothing her floral apron. "Do you take milk and sugar, young man?'

'Oh, I, er, just milk, please,' said Alan.

'I love the smell of lavender,' said Rose. 'It reminds me of my late Gran. She kept little bags of it amongst her clothes in a chest of drawers. When she'd visit us, it was like a lavender bush walking in through the front door.'

Alfred laughed. 'You're right, lass. She reeked of it something awful.'

Alan couldn't take his eyes off Rose. She was radiant. She had such rosy cheeks. Alfred noticed how flushed they were and said, 'Is this fire too warm for you two?'

'Er, no sir, thank you sir.'

Doris returned with the tea tray. Alfred didn't move. Alan jumped up to help but Doris said, 'I can manage young man. Thank you all the same.' She put the tray on the table behind the settee and asked Rose to do the honours while she decided what to order from 'Mr Kleeneze', as she called him.

'Is that stuff any good?' asked Alfred, pointing a muscular forefinger at the shoe cleaning kit. Alan handed it to him.

'The brushes look well made – better than we had in the army – I'll say that.'

'I use the polish on my shoes,' said Alan. 'It keeps the rain out and the shine lasts a long time.'

'I noticed your shoes. Very nice' said Alfred approvingly. 'Done your National Service, have you?'

'Yes sir. RAF.'

'Army man myself,' he barked, drawing his finger across his trim, grey moustache. 'Face to face with the enemy we were. Dropping bombs from an aeroplane ...'

'Dad!' said Rose, looking apologetically at Alan.

'What was it like – the First World War – fighting, I mean?'

'Horrible. It's not something you forget. It was a blood bath and it was *personal*. I still remember Helmut.'

Rose handed out the cups and offered Alan a slice of home-made apple cake. 'Did you bake this?' asked Alan. 'No. Mum. It's my Gran's old recipe.'

'Delicious,' said Alan, taking a bite and making sure any crumbs fell into his case and not onto the rug. Then turning to Rose's father, he said, 'Who was Helmut?'

'Leutnant Helmut Schneider was the German soldier I met on Christmas Day, 1914, in *no-man's land* at Ypres. Only sane day in the whole war. We stood on a 30-yard patch of ground between our trenches and sang Carols. The Jerries sang *Stille Nacht, Heilige Nacht* and we sang *Silent Night, Holy Night*. Terrible singing. Some wag said he'd rather hear gunfire.' Alan laughed.

Alfred then told how the men had exchanged presents. Handing Alan a small book, he said, 'I gave Helmut my cigarette case and he gave me this Bible.' Printed in gold lettering on the black leather cover were the words Die Bibel. 'Before I ordered my chaps back to our trenches, I shook hands with Helmut and I told him his soldiers might be tougher than mine but we'd win the war anyway.'

'When Helmut said *Nein, your men - they are tougher but vee'll vin*, I thought *Praise from my enemy is praise indeed*. When Helmut saluted and said *Aufwiedersehn*, I said *Cheerio* and saluted back. That was the last I saw of him.'

Alan noticed a faded photograph between two pages. 'That's Helmut with his wife and daughter,' said Alfred. Alan pointed to four words underlined on one of the pages: *Du sollst nicht töten*. 'Thou shalt not kill,' said Alfred. 'Thou shalt not kill! - Exodus Chapter 20 Verse 13. What a waste of life. In my book, nobody won.'

'Another cup of tea?' asked Rose.

'No thanks,' said Alan, glancing at his watch. 'I should be going.'

'Not before you take Mum's order,' said Rose. 'We've heard that Kleeneze products are better than Betterware's.'

Alan beamed. When he had written out the order – the best he'd ever had – he picked up his suitcase and shook hands firmly with Alfred who remained bolt upright in his chair. Alan wondered how he'd ever managed to sit so straight and still the whole afternoon. He thanked Doris for her order and for the tea and cake before Rose showed him to the door.

'Thanks for listening to Dad's war story. He was a major in the infantry. He lost both his legs and spent two years in a prison camp – that's where he learnt German. He never complains. He says Helmut's Bible saved his life in more ways than one.'

Alan wasn't sure what to say, so he said, 'I'll deliver your order and collect the money a week on Saturday if that's convenient.' She smiled and nodded. As he walked back down the path he thought, 'I wonder if she'd like to go to a dance?'

* * * * *

Rupert arrived early on Saturday to secure a small table by the window in The Albion before the Saturday lunchtime crowd arrived. The old-world inn, renovated in 1956, was at the end of a narrow cobbled lane. Alan assumed Rupert chose the inn for their meeting because it was close to his flat in Clifton and tucked away in a quiet spot just off Boyce's Avenue.

What'll you have?' asked Alan. 'A ploughman's and a glass of red wine with it,' replied Rupert. Alan fetched the food and drink from the bar and sat down. Their lunch consisted of four large chunks of Cheddar cheese, two pickled onions and a large freshly baked cottage roll with real butter to go with it.

'Thanks,' said Rupert, 'they do a good lunch here. My treat next time.' Then he quickly scooped his onions onto Alan's plate, saying, 'Mustn't eat these. I'm seeing the girlfriend later on.' As Alan took a sip of his orange juice, Rupert said, 'So, how did it go yesterday?'

'The best order yet. You were right. It was a doddle.'

'What did I tell you? We've got it made. After lunch we'll pop around to my flat and plan our campaign for the week.'

They ate their lunch mostly in silence. Alan only told Rupert about his order. He didn't mention Rose. He hadn't been able to stop thinking about her and couldn't wait to see her again. When they had finished eating, Rupert led the way to his flat on Sion Hill. It was warm in the sunshine so they strolled under the trees along

Rodney Place then turned left into Portland Street. 'Lived in Clifton long?' asked Alan, as they turned right into The Mall.

'About nine months.' They turned left into Gloucester Street. 'Nearly there,' said Rupert as they turned right into Sion Place. When they turned left onto Sion Hill, Alan saw the Clifton Suspension Bridge spanning the Avon Gorge.

Alan was surprised and impressed. Flat 5B Sion Hill was clean and tidy. The furniture was obviously fairly new and probably quite expensive. From the living room window he could see the famous Bristol landmark. The Suspension Bridge was designed by Isambard Kingdom Brunel in 1831 but only completed and opened for use in 1864, five years after the famous architect died.

Alan wondered how Rupert could afford to live here. Then he remembered. Rupert's mother died when he was quite young. His father - a big noise in Lloyds Bank - died not long ago. 'I've put the kettle on,' said Rupert. 'Coffee or tea?' 'Tea please.' Rupert opened the refrigerator and said, 'I haven't any milk I'm afraid.' 'Black coffee then.' Alan couldn't fail to notice that the 'fridge was empty.

They stood, coffee in hand, looking down at the road map of Bristol. They had each circled their normal sales areas – Rupert's in black and Alan's in blue. 'Wait a minute,' said Alan, pointing to one of Rupert's areas, 'another Kleeneze agent covers this area.'

'Zone!' said Rupert, 'Call it a zone.'

'Alright. Zone. It's not my zone. Another Kleeneze agent does that area - zone.'

'So, we'll concentrate on this zone to start with,' said Rupert, pointing to where the black and blue areas overlapped. With that, he used a red pen to split the 'zone' in two and labelled one half 'A' and the other half 'B'. 'On Monday and Tuesday you cover 'A' and I'll cover 'B'. On Wednesday we'll swap lists. On Thursday and Friday you do my list in zone 'B' and I'll do your list in zone 'A'.'

'What if someone wants to buy my stuff when I'm in zone 'A'?'

'That's your bonus,' said Rupert. 'Just don't forget that you're in zone 'A' Monday and Tuesday to *praise your enemy* – me - who's going to call on them Thursday and Friday.'

'I understand,' said Alan.

'Right. Got to dash. Seeing the girlfriend. Mustn't be late.'

* * * * *

For the rest of Saturday afternoon and most of the evening, Alan studied the map of his area (zone 'A') and planned his route for the coming Monday and Tuesday. At just after 5 o'clock, Rupert met a young lady coming out of Churchills music shop. She had dark curly-hair and an hour-glass figure. At her expense – she had just collected her week's wages - they had tea in a small café before occupying back seats in the Odeon cinema. Neither paid much attention to the films being shown. Rachel did some housework in the morning. In the afternoon she went for a walk across Clifton Downs and posted her letter to Jan. In the evening she listened to some classical music on the radio.

On Sunday Alan went to the morning service and skipped Evensong. In the afternoon he polished his shoes and pressed his trousers. In the evening he had a cup of cocoa with his mother and went to bed early. Rupert stayed in bed until lunchtime to recover from his late night. He treated himself to a Ploughman's lunch at the Albion with the money he'd borrowed the night before then returned to his flat to read the Sunday paper. In the evening he folded his trousers under the mattress and went to bed around 10:30 p.m. Rachel spent most of Sunday sifting through the documents and statements of accounts she had requisitioned from Lloyds Bank.

On Monday and Tuesday, Alan and Rupert put their plan into action. On Wednesday they met at 5B Sion Hill to exchange lists. Both had felt more comfortable not trying to sell their stuff and been quite surprised to have taken more orders than usual. Rupert had a tale to tell.

One rather attractive but not so young lady, wearing little more than a flimsy negligé, had invited him in and draped herself rather

40

unbecomingly across a settee. When he finished his demonstration and asked if she fancied anything he had to offer, she'd said, 'Are you trying to lead me into temptation?' Caught completely off guard for once, Rupert had replied, 'No I'm trying to deliver you from evil, madam,' and hurriedly left the house. 'I put a ring around the number of her place, old boy,' said Rupert as he gave Alan the list for his visit to zone 'B'.

'Thanks,' said Alan, 'forewarned is forearmed.'

On Thursday and Friday, they carried out the second part of their plan and were overwhelmed by its success. Customers welcomed them into their homes with open arms. The orders flowed. By Friday evening their order books were full and their fingers sore from all the writing. On Saturday they celebrated with the Chef's Special lunch at the Albion. 'My treat,' said Alan. Rupert did not protest.

'This week was just the start of better sales to come,' said Rupert. 'Hear, hear! To our future success,' toasted Alan, as they clinked their glasses. 'To better sales to come,' toasted Rupert. And indeed, in the following weeks their sales went from strength to strength. Alan then remembered that he had an order to deliver. 'Must dash,' he said and left, leaving Rupert to settle the bill for once.

* * * * *

'Rose, that nice young Mr. Kleeneze's coming up the path.' She opened the front door before Alan had a chance to ring the bell. They smiled at one another. 'Mum saw you coming,' she said. 'Please come in.' Alfred nodded. Doris beamed and said, 'You'll have a cup of tea?' When she came back from the kitchen, she gave the tray to Rose and said, 'Cut Mr. Kleeneze a piece of cake, Rose.' While the tea was being poured, Alan checked their order. 'Got my shoe cleaning kit, young man?' Alan smiled and said, 'All present and correct, sir.' When they had finished tea, Doris paid for her order with cash from her house-keeping purse. Alan thanked her again, said goodbye to Alfred and followed Rose into the hallway.

'Do you by any chance like ballroom dancing?' he stuttered. 'It's just that there's a public dance at the Victoria Rooms this evening. I wondered if you would like to go.' She turned and called out, 'Mum.' His mouth went dry. 'What is it dear?' said Doris from the sitting room. 'Do you need me this evening?' Doris appeared in the doorway. 'No. Why? Are you going out?' When Rose said she was going ballroom dancing at the Victoria Rooms, Doris beamed at Alan and said, 'What time does it start?'

As they walked down Pembroke Road that evening he said, 'Please don't call me Mr. Kleeneze. My name's Alan.' They danced well together. The band was good but a little loud. So when they weren't on the floor doing a Quickstep, a Foxtrot, a waltz or even a tango (Latin - I touch as Alan remembered from his school days), they sat in a quiet corner and talked.

Actually, it was the normally somewhat reticent Alan who did most of the talking. The evening flew by. Before he realised it, they were dancing the last waltz. And in no time at all they were at the bottom of the path of 48 Pembroke Road.

'It's been a lovely evening,' she said. 'Thank you for taking me. You're a good dancer.' Alan positively glowed. 'So are you. I *am* glad you came. Would you like to go again sometime?' His mouth was starting to go dry. 'I'd love to Alan,' she said. When the front door closed behind her, Alan's heart was pounding and he could still feel the touch of her lips on his cheek.

The next day he went to both the morning service and evensong. At the Manse after the evening service Mrs. Stockport nudged her husband and whispered, 'Alan seems very cheerful tonight.' The Rev. George Stockport whispered back, 'I think it's his new job with Kleeneze. He's out meeting people instead of being stuck in that insurance office.'

* * * * *

Their PYE (Praise Your Enemy) plan went from strength to strength. Every Wednesday they would meet for lunch to exchange lists and swap stories. Rupert usually had some rather salacious yarn to spin. Alan usually reported what Rupert called 'good deeds' like climbing a tree to rescue a customer's cat or taking a woman in labour to the maternity hospital. Both were increasing their commissions. Rupert could put food in his 'fridge and wine bottles in his rack. Alan could treat Bill and Ethel to something special for Sunday tea and put money into his Lloyds savings account. He might have saved more but somehow he always seemed to be landed with the Wednesday lunch bill.

On Saturday morning, one week after he had taken Rose dancing, Alan rang the bell at 48 Pembroke Road. Doris answered the door. 'Oh, hello Alan.'

'I just called to make sure you were satisfied with everything you ordered.'

'Everything's fine. Alfred's really pleased with his shoe cleaning kit and I just love my brushes and polish.'

'That's good. I've made a note to call when you might be running out of polish, if that's alright?'

'Were you hoping to have a word with Rose? She's out doing some shopping for me.'

'Well, I did wonder if she would like to go dancing again.'

'I'm sure she would, dear, but not tonight. She's going out.' When she saw his face, she said, 'Why don't you call her tomorrow? I'll just go a write down our telephone number.'

As he walked away with the number in his pocket, he wondered where Rose was going then told himself it was none of his business. Suddenly a thought struck him. Doris had called him Alan – not Mr. Kleeneze!

Since her visit to Holland, Rachel and Jan had corresponded regularly and frequently with picture postcards of cultural and historical interest. They were pen pals and friends - good friends but nothing more. Rachel's cards were about Bristol but she promised to send cards from Bath and Salisbury one day. Jan's cards came from

43

all over the Netherlands as he travelled to each of the twelve provinces to visit his antique shops.

In the weeks following his weekend in Amsterdam with Kate, Rupert noticed a change in Rachel. He was sure Rachel didn't know about Kate whom he was seeing regularly and more frequently than her. He wondered if Rachel's increasing coolness and reluctance to see him had anything to do with her investigations at his former bank. If it was, then he couldn't stop seeing her until she finished at the bank and he knew he was in the clear. As it happened, she had already connected the name Nicholas Spencer to certain dubious accounts. It was only a matter of time before she identified Rupert as Nicholas Spencer.

* * * * *

On Sunday Alan telephoned as Doris had suggested. 'Hello.' His heart skipped a beat and his mouth went dry. 'Hello, is that you Rose? This is Alan. How are you?'

'I'm fine, thank you Alan. How are you?'

'I'm fine.'

'Mum said you called in yesterday. I'm sorry I wasn't here.'

'So was I – sorry you weren't in I mean. Did you have a nice time?'

'If you mean last Saturday with you, then yes I did. I really did.'

'Would you like to go dancing next Saturday?'

'I'd love to but on one condition.'

'What's that?'

'You let me get the tickets. If you don't then I won't go. Pick me up at 7 o'clock.'

At two minutes to seven, Alan walked up the path and rang the bell. Doris opened the door and called upstairs, 'Alan's here Rose.'

As she came down the stairs she looked radiant. 'We won't need your car,' she said, 'we can walk to the Vic' Rooms.' Alan was a little puzzled because he knew that it was a University Student Hop and wondered how Rose managed to get tickets. He was too polite to ask.

When he walked her home after the dance he asked if she would go out with him again. 'I'd love to Alan,' she said. 'Would you like to see Quo Vadis? It's showing at the Gaumont cinema next week.' He beamed and said, 'On one condition – I get the tickets.' She laughed. 'See you next Thursday then.' She kissed him on the cheek and went indoors.

All the way home in his car he was ecstatic. He had already seen Quo Vadis – *whither goest thou* – but he would enjoy seeing it again. Peter Ustinov as Nero won a Golden Globe for best supporting actor. At the ticket kiosk, Alan chose two seats together in the middle of a row near the back of the cinema. When they were seated, he handed Rose a small box of Rowntree's Black Magic chocolates. 'Oh, thank you,' she said. 'I love dark chocolate.'

She opened the box and offered it to Alan. 'No, you first.' She took an orange cream. He had a caramel. Just in time. The lights went down and the film started. When they left the cinema, Alan took hold of her hand as they descended the steps and didn't let go until they reached 48 Pembroke Road. This time on his way home he treasured the touch of her lips on his.

In the weeks that followed, Alan and Rose met regularly not just to go the cinema or ballroom dancing. They visited the museum and art gallery. They went to a concert at the Colston Hall and an opera at the Hippodrome. They took walks across Clifton Downs. They took a boat ride up the river to Keynsham for afternoon tea. It was just after their last outing – to the Theatre Royal in King Street – that things started to go wrong.

They saw the Bristol Old Vic production of John Steinbeck's Of Mice and Men. As they left the two-hundred year-old theatre building, Alan recalled that the title of the play was taken from Ode to a Field Mouse - a poem by the Scottish poet, Robert Burns. 'Yes, you're right,' said Rose. 'it's from the seventh verse.'

But Mousie, thou art no thy lane,
In proving foresight may be vain:
The best laid schemes o' mice an' men
Gang aft agley.
An' lea'e us nought but grief an' pain,
For promis'd joy!

* * * * *

The sleet had turned to hail. The icy beads danced on the front of the car and glittered in the beam from the security lamp over the rear doorway of the church. The hailstones on the car roof provided a kind of musical accompaniment to the ballet of the bouncing ice. Alan knew he couldn't stay in the car much longer but his mind filled with the thoughts of those two life-changing weeks as he recalled the words from the Church of England Book of Common Prayer – The Burial of the Dead

> *Man that is born of woman hath but a short time to live, and is full of misery. He cometh up, and is cut down, like a flower; he fleeth as it were a shadow, and never continueth in one stay.*

* * * * *

When she entered the living room, Bill seemed to be asleep in his chair with his hands resting on the newspaper. Ethel saw his pipe lying on the floor at his feet and knew straight away that something was wrong. 'It was a heart attack,' Dr Pollard told them. 'It probably happened when he was taking a nap. He went peacefully.'

Alan arranged for the Rev. George Stockport to conduct the simple service at the crematorium and invited the few relatives and friends present to come back to the house for a cup of tea and a sandwich. Needless to say, on Monday and Tuesday of that week Alan did not cover his zone 'A' and on Wednesday he told Rupert why not.

'My condolences, old boy. How's your mother bearing up?' Then after what he thought was a suitable pause, he said, 'Here's your zone 'B' list for tomorrow.'

The same week that Bill passed away, the phone rang in Rachel's office. 'Good afternoon. May I speak with Miss Rachel Wallace please.'

'Speaking. Who is this?'

'Rachel? That is you?'

'Yes.'

'This is Lies. I am speaking from Schiedam.'

'What is it Lies? You sound upset. What's wrong?'

After a silence that seemed to last an eternity instead of a few seconds, Elise sobbed, 'It's terrible. Piet en zijn vader hebben een ongeluk gekregen.'

'Lies, I don't understand. What's happened?'

'Oh, ja, sorry. Piet and Johannes had a car accident. Piet was driving. Now he is in the hospital. His leg is broken and our hearts are broken.'

'What about Jan? Elise! Is Jan alright?'

The small 17th century Dutch Reformed Church overflowed. Close and distant relatives. Friends and neighbours. Members of the World War II resistance. People with whom he did business. People from the many charities he supported. People whom he befriended. All his employees from the twelve provincial antique shops – closed for the day. Everyone present was there to pay homage to the man they admired, loved and respected - Johannes van Dijk.

Piet hobbled into the pulpit and delivered a heart-rending eulogy. Elise gripped Rachel's hand as their eyes welled with tears. Flying out of Schipol airport back to England that evening, she opened the package Piet and Elise had given her. Inside was an envelope on which was written *for Rachel* in Jan's handwriting. Tears filled her eyes when she opened the envelope and saw the eleven postcards of Vincent van Gogh's Sun Flower paintings.

47

Rachel spent Friday in her office finalising her report on her investigations at Lloyds Bank. She was now saddened not only by the passing of her dear pen friend but also by the evidence of Rupert's role in the unscrupulous misappropriation of funds. There were those skilfully changed cheques:

Eight Thousand Pounds £8000
changed into
Eighty Thousand Pounds £80000

There were all those mortgages and account statements for people whose names she'd traced to old headstones in Arnos Vale cemetery. And there were those transfers to Swiss accounts in the name of Nicholas R. Spencer. The theft was large scale and bound to carry a heavy prison sentence. She would have to give her head of department the report on Monday. She locked it away in her filing cabinet and left the office for the weekend.

* * * * *

Alan gave what time he could spare to the list Rupert gave him for zone 'B'. Almost every visit he made yielded a substantial order even though his thoughts were elsewhere. On Saturday morning, he delivered his previous week's orders as quickly as possible then headed to George's Bookshop at the top of Park Street.

He said he'd come but Kate knew he might not. She stayed behind the counter and skipped her lunch break for fear she might miss him. She'd told him today was his last chance. She had just finished serving a customer when Rupert walked in. Kate rushed from behind the counter.

Through the window of George's bookshop Alan spotted Rupert, a short distance down the hill on the other side of Park Street, entering Churchill's Music Shop. He paid for his two books by John Steinbeck – the Grapes of Wrath and East of Eden – then hurried over to the music shop.

As he stepped inside and closed the door, he saw the dark-haired shop assistant kiss Rupert on the cheek and lead him across the showroom to the piano – a Steinway & Sons Concert Grand

48

according to the display panel alongside it. 'Play something for me,' said Kate. 'This is your last chance. When we close at five, they're loading this piano and delivering it to the maestro's home before he's back from his Amsterdam recital.'

Rupert sat down and played a few bars of Rodgers and Hart's The Lady is a Tramp. She laughed and playfully slapped his arm.

Alan walked briskly over to the piano and in a clipped tone barked, 'Begin the Beguine if you please, Corporal Coleman,'

Rupert grinned at him, played two bars then stopped. 'Sorry,' he said, 'bit rusty.'

Kate took the music from the Chappell & Co. Ltd. display in the window and put it on the piano stand in front of Rupert, saying, 'No more excuses, Ru. Here's the score.'

After the four bars of introduction, Alan, standing to Rupert's right, started singing, 'when they begin the Beguine...'

'Nice voice,' said Rupert without taking his eyes off the music. Kate, standing to Rupert's left, smiled at Alan and at the appropriate moment leant across and turned the page.

'I'm with you once more under the stars,' Alan sang.

Kate gave Rupert an adoring look as she leant over to turn the page. He smiled and winked at Alan as the music changed to the minor key.

'And there we are,' sang Alan, 'swearing to love for-ever...'

Customers gathered to listen. Rachel had entered the shop just as Kate turned the second page. She remained partly hidden behind three or four customers standing at the door. When she saw the curly, dark-haired, buxom girl kiss Rupert as she leant over to turn the third page, Rachel frowned and bit her lip.

'That's the girl I saw with Rupert at the Concertgebouw in Amsterdam,' she said to herself. When Kate put her arm around

Rupert's neck, Rachel turned and left the shop as quietly as she could.

Out of the corner of his eye Alan saw the door open. He turned to look. As the door closed he got a glimpse of Rachel's long, fair hair as she left the shop. '... till clouds come along to disperse the joys we had tasted ...'

At the end of the song Alan held the final note for the full four bars and Rupert finished with a flourishing glissando. The two men bowed to acknowledge the applause and Kate gave Rupert another big hug and kiss.

* * * * *

As she left Churchill's music shop and headed up the hill to George's Bookshop on the other side of the road at the top of Park Street, she knew what she'd have to do. The main window displayed a collection of books by John Steinbeck. Two books caught her eye and drew her into the shop. 'I'd like these two, please.'

'Oh,' said the assistant, 'Of Mice and Men. Wasn't that on at the Old Vic recently? Ah, I see this is the book. We do have the three-act play if you'd like that as well.'

When he checked the price on the other book, he said, 'Once There Was A War – it's Steinbeck's latest. I found it fascinating. It's a collection of humane and hard-hitting dispatches he filed for the New York Tribune in the Second World War. I'm sure you'll enjoy them.'

She smiled. 'I'm sure my father will. The book's for him.' He put the books and her receipt in a bag.

As he handed her the bag and her change, he said, 'Well you'll enjoy Of Mice and Men.' She smiled again and said, 'That's for my boy friend.'

Kate planted a parting kiss on Rupert's neck and went back behind the counter leaving him talking to Alan. 'Did you pick up plenty of orders this week from that list I gave you?'

'Yes. Even more than last week. What about you?'

'Same here. Another good week. You know which zones we're doing this coming week?'

'I think so. Zones 'A5' and 'B5'. Yes I'm sure.'

'That was good thinking, Alan – marking and labelling all the zones in one go.'

'Must be off. See you for lunch next Wednesday.'

When Alan had left, Rupert strolled over to the counter. 'What time this evening?'

'About half past six. I want to wash my hair first.'

'Why not do that at my place?'

'You haven't got the shampoo I use.'

'That's a poor excuse. Suit yourself. See you at six thirty.'

Rupert spotted Rachel coming out of George's and hurried to catch her up. When she heard his voice, she stopped and turned around. The first thing she noticed was the patch of red lipstick on the left side of his neck. He knew something was up when she didn't return his smile. 'Been buying me a present?' he asked. She didn't even nod or shake her head. 'Fancy a cup of tea?'

This time she nodded. 'Better get it over with,' she thought to herself. They found a table in the corner of the café & pastry shop in Queens Road. When the lady behind the counter asked what they wanted, Rachel said, 'You'll have to pay today, Rupert. I've just spent all my spare money on books.' Then seeing the notes in his bulging wallet, she said, 'By the way, I think it's about time you paid me back the money you owe me, don't you?'

When they left the café, Rachel turned left and walked towards the Victoria Rooms. Rupert turned right and headed back down Park Street. She was relieved, relaxed and considerably richer. He was anxious, tense and considerably poorer. She would have no qualms about handing in her report on Monday. That was the last they would see of each other.

When Kate saw Rupert that evening, she learned about his involvement in shady dealings at Lloyds and about Rachel. Love can turn so easily into hate. He could steal. He could take her hard-earned money. He could be fickle. Kate didn't care. But he could not tell her he'd been seeing another woman and then pretend this Rachel meant nothing to him. Kate stormed out of his flat and that was the last she saw of Rupert.

First thing on Monday morning, Rachel handed her report to her boss – the head of the Inland Revenue Investigation Department in Prince Street. 'Everything alright?' he asked. 'Never felt better,' she replied.

First thing on Monday morning, Alan took his mother to Temple Meads station to catch the train to Torquay. 'I don't like leaving you on your own, dear,' Ethel said. 'A few days by the seaside will do you the world of good, Mum,' he said. 'Don't you worry about me. Safe journey and give my love to Aunty Ruby.'

On Monday and Tuesday Alan did zone 'A5' without having to worry about his mother being in the house on her own. On Wednesday he met an unusually subdued Rupert at the Albion for lunch. 'Cheer up,' said Alan, 'it may never happen.'

'I'm afraid it already has, old boy.'

'What are you talking about?'

'No time to explain now. It's just that... well to be honest, I'm packing in this sales lark.'

'What! Why? It's going great guns.'

'Like I said, can't explain now. I've got to go away. Get away from here.'

'Why? Where are you going? How long are you going for?'

'Not sure where I'm going yet. Don't know how long for either. Might not be up to me.'

'Well that puts the tin lid on it.'

'Sorry, old boy, if this puts you in a spot.'

'The best laid schemes of mice and men gang aft agley,' murmured Alan

'What? Oh, yes – Rabbie Burns.'

'Anyway, what'll you do for money?'

'Bit of luck there. An uncle died and left me eighty thousand quid.'

'Crikey,' said Alan, '£80,000! You lucky blighter.'

'Look,' said Rupert, handing Alan a fiver, 'lunch on me today. It's been nice knowing you. Look after yourself and don't do anything I wouldn't do.'

Alan guessed that was the last he'd see of Rupert.

Early on Saturday afternoon he met Ethel at the station. She looked well. 'I'll make us a nice cup of tea, dear,' she said as they stepped inside the front door. Alan took her suitcase upstairs then joined her in the kitchen. 'Everything alright, dear?'

He took a deep breath and said, 'I'm packing in Kleeneze, Mum.' Ethel smiled and said, 'I'm sure you know best.'

Alan said, 'Yes, Mum, I do,' and smiled.

'Are you seeing your young lady this evening?'

Alan relaxed. 'Yes, Mum, I am. Is that alright? You won't mind being on your own?'

She sighed and said, 'No. I'll be fine. I've lots to do. Bill wouldn't want me sitting around moping. I'll miss him, you know, but I've got photos to look at and lots of lovely memories. You go on and enjoy yourself. You're only young once.'

* * * * *

'There's that young man of yours coming up the path,' Doris called out.

'It's Alan,' said Alfred. 'Go and let him in Doris. I'd like to show him my book.'

As she opened the door, Doris called out again, 'Rose, it's Alan. Get a move on or your dad will keep him talking for ages.'

He just had time to wave hello to Alfred before Rose rushed down the stairs and hurried him out of the house. 'You look more beautiful than ever,' he said.

'So do you,' she said with a laugh.' Alan loved the way she laughed. Nothing false about it. It was a sincere laugh. The laugh of a lovely and loving woman.

They first found a quiet corner away from the band where they could talk when they sat out a dance. Alan usually did most of the talking and realised that Rose knew far more about him than he about her. She knew, of course, he was a door-to-door salesman but he didn't know what she did for a living. She never talked about her work.

He knew she'd been in the Sixth Form at The Red Maids' School – Doris had shown him a photo of her in her red uniform – and had taken English and History. Alan took Latin and English. This evening he resolved to hold his tongue. 'Something to drink?'

She smiled. 'Let's have some wine this evening.'

When he arrived back with two glasses of wine, white for her and red for him, there was a small parcel on the little table. 'It's a present,' she said.

'Wine and now this. What's the occasion, Rose?' The band started to play.

'Open it in a minute,' she said. 'Let's dance.'

Back in their quiet corner, she raised her glass and said, 'To the future!' They klinked glasses. 'To the future,' said Alan. 'Now what's going on?'

The band struck up and she said, 'In a minute. I'll tell you in a minute.'

During the dance Alan told her that he was leaving Kleeneze. He told her about Rupert and his Praise Your Enemy plan. He told her how well it worked but how uneasy he felt about it. Then he said, 'If it hadn't been for Rupert and his PYE plan I may never have met you, Rose. I shall always be grateful to him for that.' The music stopped and they went back to their seats.

'May I open my present now?'

'Yes, dear, of course. I hope you like it.'

'Of Mice and Men – and it's the book not the play. Thank you so much, Rose.'

'Please Alan, would you mind not calling me Rose? My parents call me that because my middle name is Rosina – my grandmother's first name. I prefer my first name.'

'Sorry, I never realised you didn't like to be called Rose. So what do I call you?'

'Rachel. Please call me Rachel.'

'Not Rupert's girl? Surely not?'

'Once upon a time I may have imagined I was his girl friend. But he was never really my boy friend. And I *never* belonged to him – *not ever*.' Then for the first time in her life she was telling him things she had never told any young man, all the while afraid she might drive him away.

She did Mathematics as well as English and History at Red Maids; three A-levels not just two. '*Een knap meisje.*' She went to Bristol University and graduated with honours in Economics. '*Ja, een knap meisje.'* She worked for the Inland Revenue and had been investigating criminal activities at Lloyds Bank.

When she paused for breath, Alan, wide-eyed said, 'Crikey. In Queens Road? Rupert worked there once. Was he involved?'

'I'm afraid so but I can't discuss it.' Then the band started playing. 'Oh, Cole Porter. It's a tango.' As she got up from her seat, she said, 'Alan, it's only fair to tell you. I've fallen deeply in love.'

Alan put his right arm around her waist. Rachel took hold of his left hand. Then off they went, moving together as one to the rhythm of the music. Tango, tangere, tetigi, tactum – Latin to touch. Tangimus – We touch. As they danced, Alan sang softly into her ear, 'Strange dear, but true dear, when I'm close to you dear, the stars fill the sky...'

Then Rachel joined in. 'So in love with you am I.'

* * * * *

The sleet hadn't stopped when Alan opened the car door and made a dash for the back door into the church.

* * * * *

The evening service began as usual with a bidding prayer.

Let us pray. Let us pray for the needs of the whole world.
Let us remember those who have lost a loved one this year.
May they know peace that only You can give. Grant that our
prayers draw us closer to You and closer to those for whom
we pray. We ask this in the name of Thy Son, Jesus Christ
Our Lord. Amen.

The congregation sang the first hymn and then sat down to hear the notices. The organist played the introduction to the second hymn. The congregation rose and began to sing as the minister walked slowly up the steps into the pulpit.

The hymn ended and the congregation settled into their seats. 'In the name of the Father, the Son and the Holy Ghost,' said the

56

minister. 'Amen,' everyone said. 'My text for this evening is taken from the New Testament. Matthew - Chapter 22 - verses 36 to 40.'

"Teacher, which is the greatest commandment in the Law?" Jesus replied: " 'Love the Lord your God with all your heart and with all your soul and with all your mind.' This is the first and greatest commandment. And the second is like it: 'Love your neighbour as yourself.' All the Law and the Prophets hang on these two commandments"

The Reverend Alan 'Chalky' White paused and surveyed the congregation filling the church. When he saw Rachel Rosina, his beautiful, intelligent, pregnant wife, sitting alongside Ethel, his widowed mother, Alan smiled and began his sermon.

* * * * *

Epilogue

None of the characters bears an intentional resemblance to anyone living or dead – and that includes my friend John. I first created Rachel Wallace and Johannes van Dijk to appear in my story The Journey of a Canvas Bag. Like their thoughts, words and deeds, all the characters in this story are imaginary.

The geographical locations in which I have set their fictitious actions and the history, literature and music are real but they are drawn from memory and therefore liable to errors for which I accept full responsibility.

The bronze statue of Edmund Burke is still there in Bristol - my home town. His marble statue, at the south end of Westminster Hall in the House of Commons in London, is by William Theed. The Inland Revenue may no longer have offices in Prince Street and may never have had an Investigation Department with powers to pry behind the mighty doors of Lloyds Bank Ltd – now Lloyds TSB Bank Plc.

The Victoria Rooms housed the Student Union when I was at the University of Bristol. The Baptist Church was on the corner of East Street. There was a manse in Ackerman's Road and The Reverend George W. Sterry was a major influence on my life. It was George who advised John to stay out of the ministry if he could.

Pembroke Road and Sion Hill are real places in Bristol but the numbered locations given for where Rachel and Rupert lived are imaginary. The same goes for the home in Schiedam of my fictitious character Johannes van Dijk.

I was about to begin a year of post-graduate research in the Netherlands when I first saw Ossip Zadkine's statue Stad Zonder Hart in Rotterdam. I was moved by the statue and took the following photograph on the 14th of August 1954.

Eduard Flipse, the director of the Rotterdam Philharmonic, laid the first stone for the concert hall on the Schouwburgplein on the 9th July 1962. The first concert was performed there on the 18th May 1966. Flipse died in Breda on the 12th September 1973.

WHAT ARE THE CHANCES?

Certain people and chance events change our lives. They make us reconsider our beliefs, discard our old habits and gain a new sense of purpose and direction. This true story is about my father and an event that achieved quite the opposite. It gives credence to the adage 'Old habits die hard' and, dare I say it, to the adage 'You can't teach an old dog new tricks.' In regard to the first, I fear that I follow in my father's footsteps. Incidentally, on the North American continent a petrol cap is called a gas(oline) cap.

* * * * *

Saturday

After lunch my dad told us he was going to see the 'Robins' at Ashton Gate. The kick-off was at three o'clock. Bristol City FC (Football Club) was known locally by their nickname because the players wore bright red jerseys when they were playing at home. *Up the Robins* in those days was not derogatory but a loud shout of support. The 'City Ground' was about a mile from our house in Greville Road – a 20-minute walk away. Dad did not ask me to go with him. He knew I did not like football or walking.

At Merrywood Grammar School For Boys, I was ordered onto a soccer pitch every Wednesday afternoon, every winter and spring term, for five years. *Mens sana in corpore sano!* In my football shirt, shorts, socks (with shin pads tucked therein) and boots, I would take up my position as 'right back' and hope the ball never came my way. Whenever it did, I booted it to the other end of the field. Dad admired my strong kick but not my unwillingness to run around and get my boots muddy.

Dad loved football. In his youth he played in a league and his team were champions one season. I still have his inscribed silver medal:

Dad always came to see me play cricket for the school – I gained my colours as a Junior, Under-XIII and 1st XI – and as captain for the Bristol Schools XI. Looking back, I'm sure he would have preferred to watch me play football for the school. And to my regret, I'm sure he would have liked me to have gone with him to see the match that Saturday.

'What time are you leaving, Charlie?' my step-mother, Rose, asked.

'2 o'clock. Why?'

'Just wanted to know,' she said, giving me a conspiratorial look.

As soon as he was out of the front door, Rose said, 'What time do you think he'll be back?'

'I don't know. Match starts at 3 o'clock and lasts 90 minutes. There's an interval of 15 minutes. 10 minutes to get out of the ground and 20 minutes to walk home. I suppose he could be home by a quarter past five.'

'Play safe. Say 5 o'clock. We've got three hours.'

'What for?' I asked, guessing it was her 'royal we' and the three hours were mine alone.

'To clear out that cupboard,' she said, pointing through the window of our back room.

'Dad's junk hole in the conservatory?'

'Yes. I've got hold of some empty cardboard boxes. Put the rubbish in those and put anything worth keeping back in the cupboard. If we wait for your dad to sort out his junk, we'll be here till kingdom come.'

What my dad had in that cupboard was, as I recall, mostly junk. It is sixty years ago since I opened that cupboard on that Saturday afternoon. I remember it was full when I started and almost empty when I finished. One shelf groaned under the weight of tobacco tins filled with assorted nuts, bolts, nails and screws – all mixed in together! There was a collection of old rusty tools; several different saws, pliers and hammers – one was a panel beater's hammer which I am sure my dad never put to its intended use. I specifically remember an old spokeshave. It was blunt, very blunt, but this small two-handled plane did not get that way by my dad making wooden chair legs or spokes for a farm cart.

Another shelf was bent under the weight of paint tins whose contents varied from nearly full to practically empty. With few exceptions, the contents were solid and unusable. One or two jars were filled with brushes whose hairs were locked in a permanent embrace with the viscous linseed oil stuck to the bottom. In addition to the spokeshave, I remember quite specifically a grease gun, an oil can and a petrol cap for a car.

Rose put her head around the conservatory door and hissed, 'Quick. Your dad's back.'

'Just finished,' I said, 'closing the cupboard door.'

'Good game?' we asked. Our first mistake. He knew we weren't interested in football.

'We won for a change.' Then my dad saw us looking at one another. 'What have you two been up to?'

'Nothing, Charlie. Nothing. Fancy some bacon, egg and sausages for tea?'

'You've been up to something, I can tell.'

'I'll make a cup of tea. Would you lay the table, please, Mike?' she said, hurrying into the kitchen.

Dad took off his coat and hung it on the hook out in the hallway. When he came back into the room he must have seen, through the window, the boxes in the conservatory. The next we knew, he was out there opening the door and finding his cupboard almost empty but very tidy. Then he went for the cardboard boxes. Rose took him out a cup of tea and said, 'I asked our Mike to tidy that cupboard and throw away the junk. Don't get worked up. Drink your tea while it's hot.' Dad drank his tea, put his cup and saucer on the window sill and opened one of the boxes.

'This isn't junk,' he said, 'taking out a shiny black petrol cap. Nothing wrong with this. It might come in handy one day.'

'C.H.,' I said, 'we haven't got a car. You don't want a car. According to you, we can't afford a car. And even if we could, you reckon we couldn't afford to run it.'

'Yes, I know. But there's nothing wrong with this petrol cap. It's as good as new.'

'Dad, anybody who's got a car – a black car that this petrol cap will fit – can afford to buy a petrol cap if they lose one. Anyway, it's a screw cap, so who's going to lose one?'

'Food's ready,' called out Rose. Dad put the petrol cap in his cupboard and we went back into the house to eat.

Sunday

Dad spent the morning in the conservatory unpacking the cardboard boxes and putting most of his stuff back in his cupboard. I spent the morning in my room studying. Rose cleared away and washed up the breakfast things then read the Sunday paper before getting lunch. Early in the afternoon from my little study/bedroom I heard the front door bell. Shortly afterwards, Rose called up the stairs to say it was Jane at the door.

When I came downstairs, Jane was telling Rose and Dad that she had passed her driving test. This Sunday was the first time she had been out in the car on her own. Her father was usually with her because he taught her to drive. It was his car she was driving. We all trooped outside to see the 1939 Ford Prefect – licence plate GGK 446.

The car was black and shiny, in immaculate condition inside and out. It was brand new when her father bought it just before we declared war on Germany. It still looked brand new. The mileage on the clock was low because they hadn't been able to drive it during the war – severe petrol rationing – and because her father now only used it for pleasure on Sundays or holidays.

'So,' I said, 'this is your car now, is it?'

'No,' said Jane, 'it's my dad's. I couldn't afford to run it even if I could buy it off him.'

'Is he selling it then?

'Yes. He's had it long enough. He wants a new one.'

65

'How much does he want for it?' I asked.

'Why? Do you want to buy it?'

'I'd like to. I passed my test last year and I'm hoping to go to the States next year. I'd like to keep in practice.'

'I'd have to ask but I'm pretty sure my dad wants ninety pounds.'

To cut this long story short, Rose and I persuaded my dad to share the cost with me - £45 each. At this point I should mention that my dad was a very good and very experienced driver. He drove for a living. He began by driving a small oil lorry (or truck as it's called in North America). Then for many years he drove double decker buses. So, Jane had no hesitation in letting my dad drive us all to her house. Her mother made us a nice cup of tea while we made whatever arrangements were necessary with Jane's dad to pay for the car.

Monday

By the lunchtime, GGK 446 was parked in the road outside of our house in Greville Road. It was my dad's pride and joy. He cleaned and polished it. I looked forward to driving it to the university. I should mention here that traffic was very light in those days and parking not the serious problem it is now. That evening when my dad walked home from work – actually from the bus stop at the top of the road - we walked around our car with, I believe, a certain pride of possession. It was sixty years ago, so I cannot say for certain who spotted it first but I think it was my dad. 'The petrol cap's gone! Somebody's pinched our petrol cap!'

The rest of the story I'm sure, dear reader, you can guess. The petrol cap that my dad had taken out of the cardboard box of junk and put back in his cupboard was a shiny black petrol cap. It was also a screw cap. And it fitted GGK perfectly! From that moment on, there was nothing Rose could say to persuade my dad to throw away anything.

Epilogue

When I got married, my wife and I lived upstairs above my parents in Greville Road. We had converted my little study/bedroom into a kitchen and the front bedroom into a lounge. I bought dad's share of the car and we kept it locked safely away in a small garage at the top of the road. One year after we were married, my wife and I took GGK to Holland for a three-week camping holiday. When I took up a three-year appointment as a lecturer in educational research at Aberdeen College in Scotland, we sold the car – complete with the self-same petrol cap that dad once hoarded - in part-exchange for a newer model.

When my dad retired, he and Rose moved to the outskirts of Weston-Super-Mare to a small bungalow with its own garage. His cupboard of junk went with them. When my dad died, Rose asked me to sort out my dad's garage – she never learnt to drive – so it was my dad's garage, not theirs. The cupboard was full – mostly of junk that needed to be ditched. The problem was that I had inherited my dad's hoarding habit. With a sad heart and a head full of memories, I gritted my teeth and did Rose's bidding.

The spokeshave and any other half-decent woodworking tools went to a neighbour who would clean them and put them to good use. The tins of assorted nails and screws went to my garage. I left them behind, sorted and labelled, when we moved to Canada. The grease gun and oil can? They are sitting on a shelf in our garage in Edmonton, Alberta, patiently waiting to be used. Old habits die hard, dear reader.

A MIXED BLESSING

This story is a confession of a crime I committed out of false pride and in a moment of weakness more than forty years ago. By now both the statute of limitations and the statute of repose have probably run out and the long arm of the law in England is unlikely to reach across the Atlantic Ocean to Canada but, to be on the safe side, I ask you to believe the name of my victim and the associated geographical details to be pure fiction.

* * * * *

My father left school when he was fourteen. My mother left my father and me when I was ten. Her parting shot, when I determined to stay with my father, was that I, like him, would never amount to anything. So you can imagine my father's pride when I passed the eleven-plus examination to go to a grammar school. For most people, 1945 meant the end of World War II. For my father it meant the beginning of my seven years at Merrywood Grammar School For Boys.

To prove my mother wrong and to make my father proud, I worked hard and was more successful than I might otherwise have been. Every year I was awarded the class prize for academic achievement. Every annual speech day my proud father was there in the audience to applaud as I went onto the platform to collect my book. At my seventh speech day I was called onto the platform twice; first to receive the chemistry prize and secondly to receive the award of a University Open Scholarship.

Three years later, on the platform of the Great Hall, the Dean of the Faculty of Science in all his academic finery said, "Mr. Vice-Chancellor, I present to you Candidates to whom the Degree of Bachelor of Science has been duly awarded with Honours." The Vice-Chancellor, Sir Philip Morris, KCMG, CBE, MA, LLD, FRCS, ARCVS, replied, "By the authority of the University of Bristol, in virtue of the power vested in my office, I admit the Candidates so presented to the Degree of Bachelor of Science with Honours."

When I stepped onto the platform, wearing a rented mortar board, hood and gown which incidentally hid my dark suit – my one and only suit of any colour that I didn't rent but actually bought for the occasion - it was my father's proudest moment and the last time he would see me on such a platform.

A British Council Scholarship allowed me to undertake my first year of post-graduate research in The Netherlands in the van't Hoff Laboratorium of Utrecht University. It was there that I met Ron or, to give him his proper title at that time, Dr R H Ottewill. He was on a sabbatical term from the famous Colloid Science Laboratories at Free School Lane in Cambridge.

During our lunchtime strolls along the Catharijnesingel, a waterway near the laboratory, I learned that Ron had gained a First Class Honours degree and a Ph.D. at London University before moving to Cambridge University on a Nuffield Foundation Research Fellowship. He left London as *Doctor* Ottewill and, with another chemist - his wife Dr Ingrid Ottewill – arrived in Cambridge as *Mister* Ottewill.

Allow me at this point to explain the difference between a *proper* doctor and a *real* doctor. Ron was a *proper* doctor. He had been admitted to the degree of Doctor of Philosophy at the University of London. He was *not a real* doctor. He was not a Bachelor of Medicine registered with the General Medical Council to practice medicine. He could not sport an unbuttoned white coat, hang a stethoscope around his neck and scrawl illegible prescriptions for the sick. He was not one of the many GPs (General Practitioners) we customarily and traditionally address as Doctor even though they are not *academically* entitled to be so addressed.

Ron *was* entitled to be called Doctor Ottewill. If Ron had been a *real* doctor he might have been pleased to be called Mister Ottewill in Cambridge. Why? Because he would have joined the ranks of the medical elite and become a consultant surgeon entitled to wear a three-piece grey pin-striped suit, entitled to scare hospital registrars (junior doctors) by peering at them over half-moon spectacles and entitled to cause all female nurses – with the exception of matron – to blush whenever he appeared in their ward.

Ron was by nature modest and unassuming. Nevertheless, it rankled him to be addressed as Mr Ottewill just because he had a PhD from London and not a PhD from Cambridge. Ron soon discovered that his research as a Nuffield Fellow could, subject to *certain conditions*, form the basis of a doctoral thesis. And indeed it did. After three years at Cambridge, Ron acquired his second doctorate and became R H Ottewill BSc PhD (London) PhD (Cantab).

One of those *certain conditions* required him to live in approved accommodation and to be in by 10:30 every evening. So for three years Ron and Ingrid lived in a rented flat (apartment) which the university inspected and approved. And during those three years

71

Ingrid, officially designated Ron's landlady, was responsible for seeing that he was not out after 10:30 p.m. 'That was the only period in our lives when I was *officially* in charge and could tell my husband what to do,' said Ingrid.

Ronald Harry Ottewill went on to become an eminent chemist and Fellow of the Royal Society. Professor R H Ottewill, OBE BSc PhD PhD CChem FRSC FRS - Ron to me, to his friends and to his colleagues - died on the 4th of June 2008 at the age of 80.

Inspired by Ron to become a proper doctor, I completed my second and third year of research in Bristol where I submitted my doctoral thesis. My Viva Voce examination was conducted the day before I sailed for the USA where I remained for one year. To my father's bitter disappointment I was still in California on a Fulbright Travel Scholarship when the Dean of the Faculty of Science might have said, "Mr. Vice-Chancellor, I present to you Michael Charles Cox, Bachelor of Science of this University, to whom the Degree of Doctor of Philosophy has been duly awarded." Instead, he actually said, "Mr. Vice-Chancellor, I commend to you [*at which point he read out names from a list that included my name*] to be admitted 'in absentia' to the Degree of Doctor of Philosophy." My father was denied the opportunity to applaud his son stepping onto the platform as Mr Cox and stepping off as Dr Cox.

What, you may ask, has all this got to do with confessing my crime? It is, as a defending barrister might have submitted, '*the background needed to establish the state of mind of the defendant at the time when the crime, with which he has been charged, is said to have been committed.*' From the age of eleven I was encouraged to work hard and be proud of my achievements. At the age of twenty-five, after fourteen years of study, I was awarded a PhD and entitled to be called Dr Cox. I was a *proper* doctor and *proud* to be one.

* * * * *

At the end of my year of post-doctoral research at the University of Southern California in Los Angeles, I returned to Bristol to take the University's one-year post-graduate course in education (PGCE), to become a qualified teacher, to get a job and to get married. My fiancée was already qualified and in her first year of teaching in Bristol when Roger Wilson, the Professor of Education and my tutor, asked me if I should be interested to teach at Bristol Grammar School. I smiled when I said yes because at the tender age of eleven and to the bitter disappointment of my father and myself, I failed the preliminary entrance exam for that ancient school founded in 1532!

One Friday morning in the autumn of 1959, the headmaster, Mr John Garrett, MA (Eng. Lit. Exeter College, Oxford) informally interviewed me from behind his large desk in his large oak-panelled study. He addressed me throughout as *Mister* Cox and frequently drew attention to my *provincial* background. 'The young fellow I shall be seeing this afternoon was, unfortunately, born and bred in Cornwall but fortunately had the good sense to be educated at Cambridge,' Mr Garrett confided.

When the interview was almost at an end, Mr Garrett asked me if I had any questions to ask him. My task that weekend was to compose my first full-blown essay as part of the PGCE course, so I asked what in his opinion were the aims of education. He slumped back in his chair, clapped his hand to his forehead and exclaimed, 'I should have asked you that.'

I listened carefully hoping for some useful points for my essay entitled, as you have no doubt guessed, *The Aims of Education*. When he finished I stood up to leave.

'Well,' he said, 'Have I passed?'

'No!' I replied, looking down at him still slumped in his large leather chair behind his large desk.

'No!' he said incredulously. 'Why not?'

'You didn't answer my question. You talked about the purpose of a grammar school. I asked you for the aims of education. The two are not the same.'

As we shook hands at the door of his study, Mr Garrett warmly complimented me on my tie. When I explained that it was handwoven in pure wool in Scotland and a gift from my fiancée, he seemed to sigh as he queried, 'From your fiancée?'

'Yes,' I replied. 'We are getting married when I have completed my PGCE course. Next August as a matter of fact. On Saturday the 6th of August 1960 to be precise.' I may be mistaken but I thought the life-long bachelor seemed somewhat crestfallen at my news.

When I re-entered the headmaster's study the following Monday morning to be offered the post of assistant chemistry master, Mr Garrett said, 'Do you know, *Mister* Cox, what that wretched Cornishman asked me last Friday afternoon when I asked him if he had any questions?' I shook my head. 'He wanted to know how many points up on the Burnham scale his salary would be!' I gave Mr Garrett my best look of sympathetic horror and made a mental note to rectify my ignorance. I had never before heard of this Burnham Scale and during my interview, the question of salary had never entered my head. I also mentally concluded that my PhD would never cut any ice with *Mister* John Garrett.

After our marriage (reported in the Bristol Evening Post in a small column carrying my wife's photograph under the caption *Doctor's Bride*) and our honeymoon in Paris, my wife and I returned to Bristol, our home town. Maureen started her second year as a full-time teacher and I began my first of three years as a chemistry teacher at The Grammar School. Actually I was obliged also to teach some physics which I knew something about, to teach some biology about which I knew very little and to umpire, often on a wet and windy day, some hockey or rugby; two games which I have never understood and still have no desire to play.

When I joined the staff in September 1960, Mr Garrett, still a bachelor, had retired and been replaced by Dr John Mackay (DPhil - Merton College, Oxford); a charming man with a charming wife called Margaret. The second proper doctor on the staff was David Dickinson, the Head of Mathematics. The third and only other proper doctor was myself.

Discipline was never a problem for anybody at the school but I do believe my being referred to as *Doctor* Cox by the headmaster, the staff and the students was a factor in helping me maintain a calm atmosphere in my classroom and laboratory. I seemed to command respect from my students even though I never wore a three-piece pin-striped suit nor glared at them over half-moon spectacles. And I was, to be honest, getting quite fond of hearing *doctor* in front of my name. The PhD was beginning to be a blessing. However…

At some point during my first year of teaching, I and my colleagues were obliged to attend a parents' evening. This was a strictly formal occasion. We all wore academic black gowns and colourful hoods over our best suits. Our nameplates were mounted high on the oak panelled walls of the great hall and we sat beneath them to await any parents who might wish to see us. The high vaulted ceiling, the stained glass windows and the hushed voices around the hall created a religious atmosphere more befitting a state funeral being held in a cathedral.

While waiting patiently for my first parent, I tried unsuccessfully to eavesdrop on the whispered conversations of a nearby senior colleague. I hoped for some tips on how to conduct myself. Suddenly I became aware of a well manicured, expensively dressed lady, perhaps twenty years my senior, standing in front of me at a distance of about twelve feet. She looked up at my nameplate, looked down at me, crept to within two feet of me and peered closely at my face. She frowned.

She stepped back and once more studied the nameplate above my head. She crept forward again and whispered, '*Doctor* Cox?' I nodded. Her eyes widened. She took several steps back and shrieked at the top of her voice in a broad Yorkshire accent, 'Ee! You're just a young lad!' The Great Hall fell silent. Senior colleagues looked down their noses and junior colleagues smirked at the dent in the young *Doctor* Cox's ego.

* * * * *

After three years at the Grammar School, I applied for and was offered the post of Lecturer in Educational Research at the College of Education in Aberdeen in Scotland. I was given a three-year contract to conduct research into the latest educational innovation - Teaching Machines and Programmed Learning. Although the other candidates had the advantage of being Scottish and experienced teachers, they did not have the research background and title that came with my PhD – a blessing that outweighed my being English and inexperienced as a teacher.

After three years of marriage and full-time teaching, Maureen and I had accumulated very little in the way of furniture or money even though we lived on the upper floor of my parents' house for a modest rent. My salary when I left The Grammar School was £1050 per annum! On my new salary of £1700 per annum as a lecturer, I qualified for a mortgage on a small semi-detached house in a cul-de-sac on the edge of the city of Aberdeen.

Unfortunately before we could move in, my wife and I had to endure a very cold, very wet August month. At first we shivered in our little tent. Later we dried out and warmed up in a small caravan courtesy of the kindly Mr & Mrs Davidson, the farmer and his wife who owned the camp site and took pity on us. We were their only campers. The weather was so bad everybody else had gone home.

When the day came for us to move into our house, Mrs Davidson gave us a dining table and chairs. '*Och awa wi' ye, Doctor. Dinna thank me. We're aboot t' tak 't oot the byre tae the midden the noo. We've nae mair use for 't.*' The misinformed and prejudiced Sassenachs (we English south of the border) often portray the Scots as canny and tight-fisted and the Aberdonians as permanently bent double looking on the ground for a coin somebody may have dropped.

I did not always understand what the people north of the border were saying but I almost always found them to be friendly and generous to a fault. The exception was the couple who sold us their house. They kept postponing the completion date of our purchase. When we were eventually able to move in, there were no curtains at the windows, no carpets on the floor and no electric light bulbs anywhere! The previous owners had taken them all away.

'Good morning! My name is Dr Michael Cox. I should like an appointment to see the manager.'

'May I ask, Doctor, why ye'll be wanting to see himself?'

'I have just arrived in Aberdeen to lecture at the College of Education and I wish to open an account with your bank.'

'Certainly, Doctor. Would tomorrow morning at 10 o'clock be suitable?'

'Yes that would be fine. What is the manager's name?' I asked, before I put down the telephone.

It proved a simple matter to open an account at the Union Street Branch of Lloyds Bank and to transfer our meagre funds from our local branch of Lloyds Bank in Bristol. It also proved a simple matter to arrange an encounter with the manager. However, although my proper title gave me quick access to Alistair MacTightfist – not the manager's real name but it will suffice – it did not gain me access to his safe.

'And why would you be wanting to borrow £200, Doctor?'

'My wife wants money to buy some carpet and curtains.'

'This £200 would be in addition to your mortgage of £3250, Doctor?'

'Yes.'

'And your salary is to be £1750 per annum I believe, Doctor?'

'Yes.'

'Then I'm afraid, Doctor…'

I could detect no trace of fear in Mr MacTightfist's voice or demeanour as he confirmed the adage that *banks only lend you an umbrella when the sun is shining*. When I stepped out of the granite building into Union Street and into the rain, I had only enough cash in my pocket to buy some light bulbs. I was left with no other choice. The carpet and curtains would have to be on hire purchase (HP) – or on the never-never as my father disparagingly called it. In view of the exorbitant interest charged by the lender, I think of HP as *higher* purchase.

'Yes certainly, Doctor. Just sign here. The carpets will be delivered and fitted next week.'

'If you're going to be away for a whole week attending a conference in Oxford, I want a television set to keep me company,' said Maureen, firmly leading me from the furnishing store into a large radio and television shop in Union Street.

'Good morning, sir. May I help you?'

'Yes. My wife and I are looking for a television set.'

'Certainly, sir. Please follow me.'

The salesman led us downstairs into the basement to a bewildering array of sets. When we eventually chose a modestly priced set – a small, black & white (monochrome) CRT (cathode ray tube) television in a fake teak case – the affable salesman asked how I wished to pay. When I whispered hire purchase, he produced the necessary application forms and, without any loss of affability, prepared to fill them in. When I announced in a normal voice that I was Doctor Cox, an elderly, white-haired gentleman, seated at a desk near the foot of the stairs, looked up from his ledger.

With the paperwork completed and a delivery date agreed, my wife and I headed for the staircase. As we approached it, the white-haired gentleman was struggling to his feet. Bowing his head in my direction, he said in a reverential voice, 'Guid afternoon, Doctor.' I nodded, smiled and hurried up the stairs. I did not look back to see if he tugged his forelock. It was in Aberdeen that the penny dropped: the Scots were treating me with the respect they reserved for *real* doctors.

The tradition of medical training in Scotland began over 500 years ago and bachelors of medicine from the ancient universities of Aberdeen, Dundee, Edinburgh and Glasgow are rightly respected the world over. In Scotland itself, respect for real doctors seemed tantamount to worship. This reverence for medics was bolstered by Dr Finlay's Casebook, a popular television series broadcast by the BBC from 1962 to 1971 and by ITV from 1993 to 1996.

Dr Finlay was junior partner to Dr Cameron in his practice held in fictitious Arden House in the equally fictitious town of Tannochbrae. The two doctors were played by four celebrated Scottish actors; Bill Simpson and Andrew Cruickshank for BBC; David Rintoul and Ian Bannen for ITV. The series was based on the writings of the Scottish author, A J Cronin. When Maureen and I arrived in Aberdeen (just four months before Dr Who made his first appearance on our small screen), Dr Finlay's Casebook had been on the TV for almost a year.

* * * * *

Our first journey from Bristol to Aberdeen, a distance of approximately 500 miles (800 km), took us two days in our little black two-door 1954 Ford Anglia. Nowadays, the journey could take less than 9 hours driving most of way on the M4, M5 and M6 motorways at 70 m.p.h. However, in those days, we had to drive slowly on the narrower trunk roads such as the A6, through towns and villages often congested with traffic. So, when we saw the sign *Poplar House Bed & Breakfast* in the early evening of the first day, we were about four miles north of Penrith. We had driven just over 250 miles. We were tired and hungry.

I remember little of that first sojourn at Poplar House other than the name of the lady in charge and the names of the two villages not more than 6 miles north on the A6. The lady's name was Mrs. Heskett. I still have her card.

Mrs. Heskett

Poplar House,
Via Bowscar,
Penrith.
Tel: Plumpton (Cumberland) 230

The villages, part of the civil parish of Hesket, were (and still are) called High Hesket and Low Hesket presumably because High Hesket is about 150 feet higher above sea level than is Low Hesket.

Given the vagaries of English spelling in former times, I surmised that our hostess was descended from a long line of Hesket(t)s whose distant, foreign invading ancestors had pillaged and plundered the surrounding area from the indigenes. I gave little weight to the view that *hesket* is derived from *eski* – Old Norse meaning a place overgrown with ash trees. In my book Mrs Heskett was descended from landed gentry. She was not named after a tree. Poplar House was her country seat in Cumberland and I was determined it would be our resting place on the journeys to and fro between Aberdeen and Bristol.

'Good morning! Is that Mrs. Heskett?'

'Yes! Who is that speaking?'

'This is Doctor Cox, Mrs. Hesket. I am telephoning from Aberdeen.'

'Ah, yes. Good morning *Doctor*. How are you today?

'I'm very well, thank you, Mrs. Hesket. How are you?'

'Well enough *Doctor*. I mustn't grumble. How is your wife?'

'She's in the pink. Our daughter, Alison, is four weeks old now.'

'Please congratulate your wife for me.'

'Thank you, Mrs. Heskett. I shall. Now, may I book a room for...'

It was in the summer of 1964 that we made our first journey back to Bristol and our second visit to Poplar House. We were now a family of three. We had exchanged our small two-door Ford Anglia for a brand-new dark-green Ford Cortina. It was an estate car big enough to accommodate our daughter, all the paraphernalia a new-born baby needs - carrycot-cum-pram, bedding and clothing, feeding bottles, steriliser, innumerable nappies, etc. – and our own luggage. And as I recall, compared to the Anglia, the Cortina gave us a smoother ride and took less time to get us to the scene of my crime.

80

During our first year in Aberdeen, my wife was becoming increasingly concerned at the way people seemed to be taking me for a real doctor. She worried that I might be called upon to assist in some medical emergency. What would I do then? I supposed that I could, if called upon, apply my scant knowledge of first aid; I did have an old copy of the St. John's Ambulance *First Aid Manual* somebody had given me. In truth I had never really studied it or taken any course based on it and I no longer have it; but I do still have the *Traveller's First Aid Handbook*, A Reader's Digest guide to emergency treatment at home and abroad. This covers all major emergencies including gun shot wounds, poisoning and stab wounds. Unfortunately I only acquired it in 1985, twenty years after our last fateful visit to Poplar House when, in a moment of weakness and out of false pride, I committed my crime.

I remember there was one occasion when we did not have bed and breakfast with Mrs. Heskett. I drove from Aberdeen to Bristol in one day and took two days to recover. It was a journey none of us wished to repeat. After that we always stopped overnight at Poplar House but I do not remember exactly how many times. I do know that with each visit my wife grew progressively more unsettled by what she felt was a gradual and subtle change in Mrs Heskett's manner towards me. It was something about the way Mrs. Heskett called me *Doctor*.

'Does she know you're not a *real* doctor?'

'I don't know,' I said. 'Probably not.'

'Couldn't you get into trouble impersonating a doctor?'

'I don't *impersonate* a doctor. I *am* a doctor.'

'But you're not a *real* doctor. Mrs. Heskett thinks you are.

'I don't know what she thinks. I'm not a mind reader as you must know by now.'

'One of these days, *Doctor* Cox. One of these days…'

Before I describe *one of those days*, I should point out that the law, whether civil, common, criminal or statutory, is complex. In the UK it is mainly the Medical Acts of 1858, 1860, 1983 and 1991 that provide the statutory laws governing the medical profession, the protection of title and the right of practice. In particular, Section 49 of the 1983 Medical Act states

> *'... any person who wilfully and falsely pretends to be*
> *or takes or uses the name or title of physician, doctor*
> *of medicine, licentiate in medicine or surgery,*
> *bachelor of medicine, surgeon, general practitioner*
> *or apothecary, or any name, title, addition or*
> *description implying that he is registered under any*
> *provision of this Act, or that he is recognised by law*
> *as a physician or surgeon or licentiate in medicine or*
> *surgery or practitioner in medicine or an apothecary,*
> *shall be liable on summary conviction to a fine not*
> *exceeding level 5 on the standard scale.'*

Level 5 was £5000 when the 1983 Act came into force. It was probably less than that when I stood for that last time in the kitchen at Poplar House.

My wife waited in the doorway with our daughter in her arms as I approached Mrs. Heskett and reached out to put my money on wooden table top. 'Ee, Doctor,' said the elderly lady, placing her hand gently on my outstretched arm, 'I've been meaning t' ask you...' At that point I saw, out of the corner of my eye, Maureen flee with our baby daughter down the corridor. 'I wanted to ask you...'

'What, Mrs. Heskett?'

All of us have moments in all our lives when we are faced with a choice. We are at a junction or crossroad, if you will. Which path should we choose? Which road do we take? Such critical moments of decision often remain crystal clear in our memory and, upon reflection, are seen to be turning points in our lives. That moment, on that morning in the kitchen of Poplar House, is still fresh in my mind.

'It's my feet, Doctor. I'm having trouble with my feet.'

'Don't tell me,' I said. 'Let me guess. At the end of the day, your feet ache. They're tired. They feel hot and sore. They itch between the toes.'

'Ee, you're right, Doctor. You're quite right.'

'I'm not surprised, Mrs. Heskett, especially if you're standing on them all day.'

'Could you...'

'I interrupted with, 'I suggest you go to the local pharmacy and buy a very small amount of permanganate of potash. In the evening put one tiny crystal – just *one tiny crystal* – into a bowl of hot water. The water will turn pale pinkish purple in colour. Soak both feet in the water for about fifteen minutes. Have the water as hot as your feet can stand but be careful not to scald yourself. Try that for a while.'

'Permanganate of potash, you say, Doctor?'

'Yes. The pharmacist may call it potassium permanganate. Remember! One tiny crystal in a bowl of hot water so it's just a pale pink colour.'

'Ee, thank you, Doctor, she said.

I hurried to the car and drove away from Poplar House for the last time. My wife wanted to know what went on in the kitchen. I told her. When the judge and jury sitting alongside me in the passenger seat said that I was a criminal and should be locked up, I said in my defence, that all I did was tell Mrs. Heskett how to prepare Condy's fluid, a traditional remedy for athlete's foot – a fungal infection – and that I never once told her I was a real doctor. When my wife demanded anxiously to know what would happen to the lady's feet, I was bound to say, 'She'll have the healthiest feet in Cumberland but...' I paused and my wife gave me a worried look. '... since French polishers use Condy's fluid to stain wood, Mrs. Heskett may also have the brownest feet in the whole of Hesket!'

* * * * *

Epilogue

A J Cronin was an outstanding scholar who, in 1914, at the age of 18, entered Glasgow University to study medicine. Although his studies were interrupted by a year of naval service, Archibald Joseph Cronin became a real doctor in 1919 and a proper doctor in 1925 for his doctoral thesis on The History of Aneurism. In 1930, at the age of 34, during a three-month period of 'rest' to recuperate from a duodenal ulcer, Dr Cronin wrote Hatter's Castle, his first novel which was published by Gollancz in 1931 and made into a film in 1941. For the remaining fifty years of his life, Dr Cronin gave up practising medicine to become the celebrated novelist and dramatist A J Cronin.

Albert Schweitzer, already a celebrated organist from an Alsatian family of talented organists, began his theological studies at the University of Strasbourg in 1893, at the age 18, and six years later became a proper doctor, obtaining a PhD for his dissertation on The Religious Philosophy of Kant. In Strasbourg, as Dr Schweitzer, he preached at the church of St. Nicholas, worked as an administrator at St. Thomas Theological College and published his famous book The Quest of the Historical Jesus and other books including a biography of Bach. In 1905, at the age of 30, Schweitzer began studying medicine. When he became a real doctor, Schweitzer went as a medical missionary to French Equatorial Africa where he founded a hospital in Lambaréné. In 1952 he was awarded the Nobel Peace Prize; he used the money to start a leprosarium.

In 1963, on the 23rd of November, the English actor William Hartnell starred in the first episode of the BBC Television science fiction series Dr Who. Thanks to his regenerative ability as a Time Lord, the fictitious Dr Who has already been portrayed by eleven different actors. The series ran continuously until 1989 and was regenerated by BBC Wales in 2005. The twelfth Dr Who appeared in the eighth series that started in August 2014. There seems to be no end in sight for Dr Who but the fictional Dr Cameron and Dr Finlay are long forgotten. Sadly I suspect that most people today will know more about the fictional Dr Who than they do about those two real and proper distinguished doctors, Archibald Cronin and Albert Schweitzer.

I am still Dr Cox, a proper doctor, but to avoid any risk of lawsuits I always explain to new acquaintances that should they faint and fall to the ground, all I could do is to jump over them and fetch a real doctor.

THE LAWNMOWER

This is a true story. By that I mean I have described a real incident to the best of my ability and memory. However, I have not disclosed the names of the real people involved. Any former friends and neighbours who think they recognise themselves and take exception to being excluded or included will, I trust, accept my apologies and neither strike me from their Christmas card list nor add me to their to-be-sued list.

* * * * *

'It's probably nothing,' she said with a look on her face that suggested she thought otherwise. 'Anyway, I'm playing safe and reporting to you, Colonel.'

Ours was a quiet little horseshoe-shaped cul-de-sac of nine individual dwellings in a quiet little village barely three miles from the Dorset coast. My wife and I lived at number 2 for fifteen years before I retired. During that time, the only reported incident was a quiet break-in at number 3 when thieves quietly jemmied the rear patio door and quietly stole Joyce's jewellery. In point of fact there were two incidents because, true to form, the thieves returned to number 3 just after the rear door was repaired and quietly stole Martin's collection of silverware.

Just after I retired, I was unanimously elected to organise a neighbourhood watch for our cul-de-sac and to be its representative. Gerald Thompson, the wag at number 5, gleefully christened me Colonel of the Watch! He may have been thinking of his prize possession, an original cartoon - signed by the cartoonist, Sir David Low himself - showing Colonel Blimp naked, save for a towel around his waist, and spouting nonsense in a Turkish bath. Then again he may not have had Blimp in mind. I'm not bald or fat. I do not frequent steam baths. And I consider myself neither pompous nor reactionary. That said, Mrs Margaret Drummond at number 6 would be quick to knock me sideways with a quote from a poem by her countryman, Robert Burns:

"O wad some Power the giftie gie us, To see oursels as ithers see us!"

So, here I was retired and Colonel of our Neighbourhood Watch. What was I supposed to do? Well, first of all I had to persuade the local authority to install an official sign:

THIS IS A NEIGHBOURHOOD WATCH AREA

In the fullness of bureaucratic time, it was installed without pomp or ceremony high up on our street lamp. It is still there as far as I know. Does it deter would-be burglars? Perhaps! However, they would need better eyesight than Don Grant at number 9 who never saw the sign until Barry Whiteside, at number 7, pointed it out. And of course they would have to take the road into our cul-de-sac and not quietly sneak down the lane at the back of numbers 3, 4 and 5.

What was left for me to do once the sign was installed? Listen from time to time to the recorded telephone messages from the local police station and pass the information to the residents in our cul-de-sac.

A bicycle has been stolen from a garden shed in Clarendon Close. Residents are advised to keep sheds locked and any windows covered to conceal the contents from prying eyes…

Apart from those two quiet burglaries at number 3, which occurred before we formed our neighbourhood watch and before the local authority workman put up our sign, nothing untoward happened until that fateful Saturday morning when Mavis Birch from number 4 rang my doorbell.

* * * * *

'Is that the postman?' inquired my wife, Maureen, from the kitchen.

'No, my dear. It's Mavis.'

'Who?'

'Mavis Birch from number 4.'

'I'll be out in a minute.'

'Don't bother, dear. It's neighbourhood watch business. I shan't be long.'

'Hello Mavis,' said my wife, brushing past me. 'I'm just making coffee. Fancy a cup?'

'That would be lovely. Thanks.'

'Black and no sugar?'

'Please.'

'Come on in and make yourself at home. Michael! Take Mavis into the lounge. I'll fetch the coffee.'

Mavis had barely dropped her sparse, bony frame into the contrasting ample, soft padding of my favourite easy chair when Maureen appeared with the coffee and biscuits. 'Michael! Come away from the window and offer Mavis a biscuit while I pour the coffees.' I did as I was told. 'Try the one wrapped in foil, Mavis. It's milk chocolate with an orange-cream filling.' For one moment I thought I was going to lose my favourite biscuit as well as my chair but true to form, Mavis shook her head and muttered something about watching her weight. As far as I could tell, she was the last person who needed to do that but I admit I was grateful for her watchfulness.

I extracted my chocolate biscuit from its protective foil, took a bite and waited for a lull in their conversation.

'What did you come to report, Mavis?' I interjected at the least inconvenient moment.

'Oh, it's probably nothing really,' she replied. 'It's just that...'

'Something suspicious?' Maureen said.

'Not suspicious. Just a bit odd, I suppose. A bit unusual...'

'Well, go on,' said Maureen. 'Tell us all about it.'

'It's Martin's lawnmower.'

'Martin Lake at number 3; his lawnmower you mean?' I asked.

'Yes,' said Mavis, turning again to look at Maureen. 'You know Martin? He and Joyce live right next door to me. Lovely couple! They were very sympathetic when Aubrey left me.'

'What about Martin's lawnmower, Mavis?' I asked, seeing her eyes starting to well up and fearing the effect a loss of even a few tears might have on her body weight.

'Oh, yes. Sorry!' said Mavis, dabbing the corner of her eyes with a lace handkerchief. 'I heard its engine running but it didn't sound right.'

'What do you mean, Mavis?' asked Maureen. 'It didn't sound right.'

'The engine was making a loud, high-pitched noise. I think,' said Mavis, looking at me,

'Sounds like it was racing,' I said.

'Racing? I don't know what you mean?' said Maureen, looking at me.

'Revving an engine so it's running too fast for the gear it's in,' I said looking at my wife. 'It's what set your father's false teeth on edge when he was trying to teach your mother to drive.'

Mavis gave a sympathetic glance in Maureen's direction then said, 'It's not just that the engine was racing. The mower wasn't cutting the grass. It was just standing there.'

'Sorry, but you've lost me, Mavis,' I said. 'Standing where?'

'I think you should come and take a look.'

* * * * *

We finished our coffee and followed Mavis into the cul-de-sac and up the steep drive to the front of number 3. As we climbed the steps to the terrace and front door we could hear the high-pitched whine of the lawnmower. The noise was coming from the side of the bungalow. When we reached the metal gate barring the way to the path to the rear garden, we saw the screeching mower belching smoke for all it was worth. It was alongside the wide-open door of Martin's garden shed.

'It was just like this twenty minutes ago, Colonel, before I came to make my report.'

'So it's been running for at least twenty minutes?'

'More like thirty minutes. I only came to look after I finished hanging out my washing.'

'Joyce probably called Martin indoors for some reason or other,' I said. 'lost track of time and forgot that he'd left the engine running. Did you ring their front door bell?'

'Actually, no I didn't. I was afraid they would think I was being nosy. They probably wouldn't think that if the Colonel of our Neighbourhood Watch rang their bell'

Maureen and Mavis studied the pots of flowers and shrubs on the terrace whilst I rang the front door bell. There was no response. I rang several times. There was no sound of movement inside the bungalow. I peeped through the letterbox. The place seemed deserted. I opened the side gate – normally padlocked shut – and walked to the back of the bungalow and peered through all the windows. The place was deserted. I returned to the front terrace to find that Don Grant, from number 9, had joined Mavis and my wife.

Don was, as usual, dressed in his one-piece blue work overall, the embroidered insignia, BEC, on the left breast pocket identifying his former employers as the Bradford Engineering Company. On his head was a red hard hat to which was clamped a pair of large, yellow ear defenders. Below the rim of the hat, his long, collar-length, swept-back grey hair was held in place by the elastic strap of the safety goggles that protected his steel-rimmed prescription spectacles. Around his nose and mouth I could see the marks of the formidable dust mask that now hung under his chin. The shiny black industrial gloves protruding from the sleeves of his overalls and the matching industrial boots peeping from beneath the trouser legs completed the picture of a worker ready for any eventuality.

'Good morning, Don. Nice morning,' I said pleasantly.

'Something up?' said Don curtly, fixing me with his doubly protected beady eyes.

'It's Martin's lawnmower,' said Mavis. 'It's…'

Don didn't wait for Mavis to finish. He hurried to the side of the bungalow and pushed open the gate. The three of us followed.

'Martin should know better than to rev the engine like this. Bad for the cylinder.' said Don, delicately adjusting the throttle until, like a tuner preparing a grand piano for a concert, he was satisfied with the note.

'Well done,' said Maureen. 'You've certainly cut down the noise. Martin will be pleased.'

'He might,' I said with little conviction in my voice as I tried to imagine my reaction if Don had fiddled with my lawnmower without so much as a by your leave.

'You won't get any more soot on your washing now, Mavis,' said Maureen.

'Right,' said Don, turning towards the gate. 'That's that problem solved.

'Actually,' said Mavis, hesitantly, 'that was only part of the problem.'

'The fact is,' I said, 'Mavis, found the lawnmower running full blast thirty minutes ago and reported to me. The three of us came to investigate and as far as we can tell the bungalow is deserted. There's no one at home.'

According to his wife Mary, Don Grant didn't actually retire several years ago. BEC made him redundant. Mary, Don, his mother Edie and his large parrot, Cracker, left Bradford as soon as they could to set up home in the small bungalow – at number 9 - in our cul-de-sac in Dorset. Over the years, Don extended and modified their detached double garage until, from the outside, it looked less like a garage and more like a larger version of their bungalow. The garage now held his old car, a boat that had never been on the water, two large workshops equipped with an assortment of industrial machinery and a large wood-burning stove to keep everything warm and dry in winter.

Each day Don behaves as though he had never stopped work. He walks the few steps from his home to his place of work, his garage, where he puts on his overalls and safety gear before checking the daily job sheet on his clipboard. The jobs vary from designing & installing a system for collecting & storing rainwater to trimming the leylandii hedges. And all these jobs, including trimming the hedges, he does with an engineer's precision – to the nearest thousandth of an inch. Suffice it to say, Don is a confident, practical man with a down-to-earth approach to life's problems.

'Where's Don off to?' said Maureen.

'I imagine he's going to ring the door bell, peer through the front and back windows to check for himself that the bungalow is empty.'

'There's no one home.' said Don, 'I checked.' I gave Maureen a look to stop her saying I'd told him that. 'The front and back doors are locked so I couldn't go in to check the back room where the curtains are still pulled.'

'Why would you want to do that?' asked Mavis nervously. 'What are you thinking?'

'Well,' said Don, 'let's face it, Martin's not very practical. Perhaps there's been a gas leak and the two of them are lying in bed unconscious, maybe even dead.'

'Oh dear, do you think so?' said Mavis, looking at me.

'I didn't smell gas when I looked through their letter box,' I said. 'I'm sure there's nothing to worry about. They've probably just popped out and Martin forgot all about the lawnmower.'

'What's going on?' Why are you all up here?' It was Don's wife, Mary.

'Martin's lawnmower was making a racket alongside the house and there's no sign of Martin or Joyce.' I told her.

They've gone out,' said Mary.

'How do you know that?' Maureen asked.

'I'm pretty sure I saw Joyce drive down the road this morning,' Mary replied.

'Joyce was driving?' I asked. 'Not Martin?'

'Yes, I'm pretty sure it was Joyce.'

'And Martin was in the passenger seat?' I queried.

'Oh, well I'm not sure about that. Joyce was definitely driving. Martin might have been sitting alongside her. I don't know. He is tall but he's got very long legs. With his short body he could have been hiding behind Joyce.'

'It's a bit odd if they were both in the car but Joyce was driving,' I said. 'When they go out together, Martin usually drives.'

Martin and Joyce were the oldest retired couple in our neighbourhood watch. Martin had been a highly respected senior orthopaedic surgeon. Joyce was a highly qualified State Registered Nurse (SRN) who served for many years as matron in a major hospital. Contrary to what Don had said, Martin was a fairly handy

93

man but in his own unorthodox way. For example, I remember an occasion when I saw Martin on his hands and knees doing something at the base of a very large but dead tree. I walked up the drive to see what he was doing. Don quickly joined me.

'What are you up to now, Martin?' I asked

'This tree has had it. I'm cutting it down.'

'With that miniature hacksaw?' asked Don, in utter disbelief.

'Yes, why not?' said Martin with a wicked smile.

'You need my chain saw,' said Don.

'No thank you,' said Martin. 'I can manage perfectly well with this. I just scrape away the soil, find a root and amputate it with my hacksaw. I grant you it's a bit slow and tedious but when I've cut all the roots, the tree will fall down.'

We left him to it. An hour or two later, to Don's chagrin, the dead tree fell over. Personally I shouldn't have been surprised if Martin had used his surgeon's scalpel instead of that mini-hacksaw. Needless to say, at Martin's request, Don returned later with his chain saw, cut the tree into logs and hauled them away for his stove.

* * * * *

While we were waiting at the top of the drive for Don to try unsuccessfully to look into Martin's garage to see if one of their cars had gone, Mavis's neighbours, Brenda and Gerald Thompson joined our group.

'Morning Colonel,' chirped Gerry, giving me an exaggerated salute. 'Laying siege to number 3, are we?'

'As a matter of fact,' I began, 'we are...'

'We're worried about Joyce and Martin,' said Mavis. 'Don thinks they may have been gassed.'

'How terrible!' said Brenda. 'How did it happen?'

94

'Look here,' I said, trying to take control of the situation. 'That's not quite what Don said. He said there may have been a gas leak and Martin and Joyce may be lying in their bed unconscious.'

'Have you called the police, Colonel?'

'No! I haven't, Gerry, because…'

'Shall I call them?' asked Gerry, producing his mobile phone from the leather case attached to his belt.

'No! Definitely not,' I said. 'There's been no gas leak. Nobody's unconscious. It's just that Martin and Joyce are nowhere to be found and…'

'I think they've popped out to the shops,' said Mary. 'They usually go shopping on Saturday morning although I can't think why now they're retired. Monday's much better. It's less crowded.'

'Yes but the vegetables are often fresher on Saturdays,' said Maureen authoritatively.

'I agree,' said Brenda.

'Look here,' I said, trying again to take control. 'The fact is Martin's lawnmower was left running at the side of the house, we can't find Martin or Joyce and Mary thinks she saw Joyce drive down the road but she's not sure if Martin was in the passenger seat.'

'I saw Joyce's car go down their drive about half an hour ago,' said Brenda.

'Joyce's car? Not Martin's?' I asked.

'I think it was Joyce's,' said Brenda.

'Was Martin with her?' Maureen asked.

'I've no idea,' said Brenda.

'The point is,' I said, 'if Martin was with Joyce, why wasn't he driving?'

'And why was she driving Martin in her car?' Gerry chipped in.

* * * * *

For no particular reason, other than perhaps the thought in the back of my mind that Martin and Joyce might return at any moment and not be pleased to see the seven of us barring the way to their garage, I started to walk down the drive. The others followed me across the cul-de-sac to gather outside Don and Mary's house. Mrs Margaret Drummond probably saw the procession from her kitchen window. She hurried down her drive to be joined by Barry and Sheila Whiteside from number 7.

When Margaret married, she moved with her husband to the Midlands where he launched what was to become a very successful business. She had four children, three boys and a girl. When the oldest boy was eleven years of age, Margaret's husband died. She was left to bring up her four children and to run the business. When she retired and came to live in Dorset, her daughter had become a State Registered Nurse and her three sons had graduated from Oxford University, one becoming a barrister, another becoming a surgeon and the third becoming a mathematician.

None of us knew Margaret's age. Her thick, well groomed white hair gave her the appearance of the senior she probably was but her boundless energy was that of someone much younger. She did her own gardening and the results put us all to shame. She changed her car regularly because she drove thousands of miles each year visiting family and friends and dealing with business matters. She employed an accountant to handle her financial affairs so that she could voluntarily manage the local Citizens Advice Bureau. Mrs Margaret Drummond was a formidable lady.

'Might I ask what's going on?'

'Good morning Mrs Drummond,' I said. 'Nothing is actually going on. It's just that Martin Lake's lawnmower was left running at the side of their bungalow and Martin and Joyce are nowhere to be found. Mary says she saw Joyce drive down the road this morning and Martin may have been in the passenger seat. If Martin was in the car, we're wondering why he wasn't driving.'

'Presumably,' said Mrs Drummond, 'because he wasn't fit to drive.'

'Bit early in the morning for Martin to be hitting the bottle wouldn't you say?'

'That's not what I meant, Mr Thompson,' retorted Mrs Drummond. 'Mr Martin Lake is certainly a connoisseur of fine wine but he is certainly not given to overindulgence at any time of the day or night.'

'What did you mean, Mrs Drummond, when you said Dr Lake, sorry, when you said Mr Lake may not have been fit to drive?'

'That he was unwell. Taken ill, if you prefer.'

'So where was Joyce taking him?' Barry Whiteside asked.

'Hospital!' stated Mrs Drummond in a matter of fact voice. 'Where else?'

At that, separate little conversations broke out. Mavis recounted to Barry the events of the morning, including Don's theory that Martin and Joyce may have been overcome by a gas leak. Brenda admired Mrs Drummond's sweater and discovered that it actually was from Fair Isle and was hand-knitted by a man or woman in the Shetland Isles. Gerry pulled Don's leg by asking him if he really needed all this protective gear just to replace a washer on a tap. Brenda, Mary and Sheila discussed the pros and cons of vegetable shopping on Mondays instead of Saturdays.

'Mrs Drummond could be right, you know. Joyce could have rushed Martin off to hospital,' I said, drawing Maureen aside.

'Why do you think that?' whispered Maureen.

'Well, I know Martin is slim and looks as fit as Barry Whiteside who's probably 15 years younger and always playing golf with his wife and Tony and Josie. But, I do know Martin's been on the receiving end of the surgeon's scalpel quite a few times in the past.'

'Really?'

'Oh yes! And,' I confided, leaning forward to whisper in Maureen's ear, 'he suffers from arrhythmia.'

'Meaning?'

'A dicky ticker, old girl.'

'So Martin might have had a heart attack. Is that what you're saying?' Maureen asked.

Before I could reply, someone tapped me on the shoulder. It was our neighbour, Ray, from number 1. His wife Pat had joined Brenda, Mary and Sheila to discuss Saturday grocery shopping.

'Hello Ray,' I said, smiling. 'What brings you out of the house?'

'Pat and I wondered what the gathering's all about. Anything to do with the mess the Council has made of our road and footpath?

'Well, no. As a matter of fact…'

'Damn disgrace.' said Ray. 'They did a first class job when they resurfaced our road and pavement, right?' I nodded in agreement. 'But then what? Days later, the Electricity Board dig holes everywhere. They're no sooner gone than the Gas Board comes and dig more holes.'

'Terrible!' said Maureen. 'You'd think that…'

'After the Gas Board we had the Water Board digging more holes. God only knows why. Last week British Telecom dug their holes. It wouldn't be so bad but not one hole was filled in properly. One of these days one of us is going to trip and break something. Then who's to blame? We'll never be able to prove who dug and refilled the hole we tripped over. And you can forget taking the Borough Council to court. It just would be a waste of time and money. All because someone in the Highways Department can't arrange for our road and pavement to be resurfaced after these idiots had dug their holes. Why if I had my way…'

'Ray! Have you heard? Martin Lake's in hospital.' It was Ray's wife, Pat. 'Don Grant thinks he may have been gassed.'

* * * * *

Things were definitely getting out of hand. There was now quite a crowd outside the Grant's bungalow. Apart from Martin and Joyce Lake, the only people missing were Josie and Tony Small from number 8. Just as that was going through my mind, their black BMW tore around the corner into our cul-de-sac, its sudden appearance and speed being enough to make anybody standing in the road jump onto the footpath and form a line along its edge. Maureen exchanged raised-eyebrow glances with Sheila; they frequently feared for the safety of their Persian cats that often sat in the middle of the road preening themselves in the sunshine.

I didn't want Tony and Josie being fed any misinformation, so I hurried to meet them as they came to join the throng.

'Quite a get-together,' said Tony. 'Have you called a meeting, Colonel?'

'No, not at all. It all started when Mavis came to tell me about Martin's lawnmower.'

'Sawbones Martin?'

'Mr Lake,' I said loudly, hoping Mrs Drummond hadn't overheard Tony, 'has disappeared. Joyce might have taken him to hospital.'

'Do we know what's wrong with him?' Josie asked.

'We don't know there's anything wrong with Martin,' I said. 'It's just a theory.'

'So what's this got to do with his lawnmower?' Tony asked.

99

'Mavis found it standing alongside Martin's garden shed. It had been left running at full throttle and belching smoke. The shed door was wide open and the metal gate was unlocked. We rang their front doorbell and looked in all the windows but the bungalow was deserted. There was no sign of Martin or Joyce anywhere.'

'Well, you're in charge,' said Tony. 'What are you going to do?'

I was about to confess that I had no idea what to do, when Barry shouted out, 'Your boy's goats are on the loose again, Gerry.' Sure enough, two goats were heading across the front lawn towards number 6. Young Stanley Thompson was in hot pursuit of his pets. A cheer went up when the teenager grabbed their collars just before they reached Mrs Drummond's garden. 'I thought your dahlias were done for this time, Margaret,' said Barry, with a grin all over his face, obviously impervious to the scowl she gave him.

'I'm surprised that you are allowed to keep goats or any other livestock on your land, Gerald,' said Mrs Drummond. 'Our land is subject to a restrictive covenant. It dates back to Lord Shaftesbury's time. If we're not allowed to keep caravans here, I cannot imagine the Council allowing your goats and chickens or Don's parrot.'

'Actually,' said Gerry, 'They're not my goats. They're Stanley's. Anyway, Lord Shaftesbury's been dead awhile, so I really don't think he'll be bothered. And unless somebody complains, I don't think the Borough Council will be bothered either.'

Before Gerry and Mrs Drummond could say any more to one another I stepped in and asked how Stanley was doing now he had left school. Brenda told us that during the day he worked at the wholesale animal feed company on the quayside and that in the evenings he was studying hard to retake his exams and improve his results.

'Good for him,' said Mrs Drummond. 'Any idea what he wants to do afterwards?'

'Breed goats,' said Gerry, shaking his head in disapproval. 'That's why he's got this pair.'

'Perhaps he'll change his mind when he passes his exams and goes to university.'

'If he passes.' said Gerry. 'And if he decides to apply to university.'

'Has he thought of reading veterinary science?' asked Mrs Drummond.

'Unfortunately,' said Gerry, 'he dropped sciences in favour of English and History.'

* * * * *

We were all so distracted by Stanley's pair of rare Bagot goats that we nearly didn't notice Joyce's car turn into the cul-de-sac and drive slowly past the line of people. As she went by, everybody started waving and smiling. She looked completely bewildered. I imagine she thought we'd all gone mad. She didn't stop. She just drove up her drive and parked in front of her garage.

'Where's Martin?' someone asked.

'He wasn't in the car.' said someone else.

'I think you should go and have a word with Joyce,' said Maureen. 'Find out what's happened.'

'Yes, go on,' said Gerry. 'You're our leader. Ask her where Martin is.'

'Somebody looking for me?' It was Martin Lake. He had walked unnoticed into the cul-de-sac and joined the end of the line.

'Good Lord, Martin!' I said. 'Where have you come from? Are you OK?'

'We've all being terribly worried,' said Maureen.

'Don thought you and Joyce might be dead, gassed in your bed,' exclaimed Mavis.

We all gathered round while Martin explained what had happened. Joyce wanted to go shopping in the town. He wanted to change his library book so Joyce gave him a lift into the village. It was a nice morning so he decided to walk home.

'What about your lawnmower?' asked Don. 'Did you know you left the engine running?'

'Oh yes,' said Martin. 'I didn't want to put it away in the shed for winter with fuel still in the tank. Wouldn't want to risk a fire.'

'But you could have ruined the engine,' said Don.

'I doubt it!' said Martin. 'I've been doing this for the past ten years without much damage as far as I can tell.'

'Why did you leave your side gate and shed unlocked?' I asked.

'Why not? There are only a few old garden tools in the shed - nothing worth stealing. Besides, if thieves can break into our securely locked bungalow and steal our valuables, they'll make short work of a padlock on a shed door.'

After the crowd had dispersed, I expressed my relief that he had not been rushed into hospital on account of his arrhythmia. Martin gave me a somewhat superior kind of look, one that a surgeon might give a young student doctor, and said in a matter of fact voice, 'There are many types of arrhythmias. Mine are premature atrial contractions - early extra beats that originate in the atria or upper chambers of the heart. They're quite harmless and require no treatment. Now if you'll excuse me, Michael, I'd better go and help Joyce unload the shopping.'

* * * * *

Epilogue

In 1982, the United Kingdom of Great Britain and Northern Ireland saw the launch of satellite TV, the start of the Falklands War and, in the sleepy village of Mollington near Chester, the formation of the first neighbourhood watch. One of the villagers brought back the idea from a visit to the USA and Canada.

In April 2009 in the UK there were 133,195 neighbourhood watch schemes registered for Public Liability Insurance (PLI) and covering more than 7½ million households. It is estimated that schemes not registered for PLI would increase the number to more than 170,000 neighbourhood watch groups with over 10 million members.

We did form a neighbourhood watch in the cul-de-sac in Dorset where we lived and thereby encouraged a greater neighbourliness and a closer community spirit. I was called the 'Colonel' and my neighbour did leave his lawnmower running and cause us all great concern.

David Low, the political cartoonist and satirist, was born in New Zealand in 1891. He came to London in 1919. Colonel Blimp, his most famous character, was created in 1934 to represent a pompous, reactionary, ultra-nationalistic person. David Low was knighted in 1962 and died the next year.

The caption in this cartoon is: "Gad, Sir, There! Non-intervention! Away with the warlike League of Nations! Why doesn't the Gov't send the Fleet to protect our investments in China?"

Stanley Thompson – that's not his real name – did keep a pair of goats and intended to breed them but they may or may not have been Bagot goats, a breed in existence since 1380 and named after the family then living in Blithfield Hall, Staffordshire. However, Stanley retook his exams after he left school, went to university and obtained a degree in English and went on to study law. He is now a successful barrister living in London.

Keep reading for an excerpt from the first story in Volume 3 of Michael C. Cox's collection of short stories

Facts and Fantasies

available from Amazon as an individual volume or part of the

Omnibus Collection of Short Stories

in paperback and electronic book form

* * * * *

DECEPTION AND A DEADLY SWITCH

The truth underlying this story is the foolish unsecured loans that two colleagues and I made to a former colleague and his brother in 1991. The name of the school, the names of the two companies and the names of the characters, apart from my own, are fictitious. I definitely lost money. I believe I was deceived. I think it best not to comment further.

* * * * *

The two men shook hands and parted. I saw them as I happened to glance out of the window of my classroom, on the upper floor of the school, overlooking the car park. What, I wondered, was Cyril Rainsthorp doing shaking hands with a dubious former member of staff? Even with senior colleagues such as myself, our Head of Classics refused to shake hands in order to minimise the risk of contagion – one of his favourite words derived, as he never hesitated to declaim, from the Latin verbs *tangere*: to touch and *contingere*: to touch on all sides or pollute.

My thoughts were interrupted by the bell to end morning school. As I reached the foot of the staircase, Cyril came through the main door into the foyer. The cold wind had brought a pinkish colour to his sallow cheeks and made his white hair even more dishevelled than usual. We walked side-by-side down the corridor to the staff common room.

'I thought I saw A Simpleton in the car park just now getting into a new red Mercedes.'

'Sorry, I'm not with you, old boy,' replied Cyril, giving me a sideways squint.

'Anthony Simpleton. Unfortunate name for a schoolmaster. Left here about three years ago to set up his own computer business.'

'Oh, I didn't know his first name was Anthony,' said Cyril, unconvincingly.

'Tony! Most of us called him Tony.'

'Oh! I didn't really know him. What did he teach?' he asked, seemingly without interest.

'Physics and mathematics.'

'Ah! I see. Bit of a boffin then? Clever chap was he?'

'Tony always thought so. Probably still full of himself.'

'I'm surprised a clever chap like that hasn't changed his surname by deed poll.'

'He seemed to take a perverted delight in his name,' I said. 'Did you know his middle name is Simon?'

'A worthy name. Two of the Apostles were called Simon.'

'True. Unfortunately, some of our rather less worthy pupils favoured the association of Simon with the nursery rhyme: *Simple Simon met a pieman going to the fair...*' I said, tailing off, not knowing the rest.

'*Said Simple Simon to the pieman, Let me taste your ware,*' continued Cyril. '*Said the pieman to Simple Simon, Show me first your penny. Said Simple Simon to the pieman, Sir, I have not any.*'

'Bad enough that our wretched pupils nicknamed him Simple Simon,' I remarked, 'Do you recall how quick our colleagues were to draw attention to his initials when the draft timetable was posted on the notice board.'

'His initials? Oh, good gracious!' exclaimed Cyril as the penny dropped. 'ASS! But...'

'Indeed. Fortunately our beloved headmaster had them changed to TSS. The mind boggles at what the Upper Fifths might have made of ASS.

It was in 1983 that Tony Simpleton began his five-year teaching career at Lytchett Upper, our minor league independent boarding school for boys. During that period, Dr Trevelyan Wynne Evans, our fiery headmaster and former Welsh Rugby International, would from time to time ask me as chairman of the staff common room and Head of Science what I thought of Tony as a colleague and teacher. Trevelyan and I were a similar age and hoping to retire early. The staff saw us as the elderly bastions of the old school, being of one mind on the subject of *discipline* (masters were paid to teach and pupils were required to learn) and *uniforms* (blazers and badges for the boys; suits, ties and gowns for their masters).

Tony did wear a suit. It may have been a good fit once upon a time. We only ever saw the coat buttoned up at Sunday morning chapel. Tony's considerable bulk was a possible benefit when he was on the field in rugby kit but the bulge around his middle (courtesy of the ale he drank at the local village tavern) was an unequivocal deficit when he was straining his voice and the buttons of his suit in the staff pews.

Over the summer holiday between his first and second year at the school, Tony grew a thick beard. Staff opinion on it was divided. The geographers, grammarians and scientists said he grew it to compensate for his advancing alopecia. The classicists, historians and linguists said he wanted to hide his youthful features. A small minority which included myself and, I suspect, Dr Evans, believed he grew the beard to make it hard for us to tell if he was wearing a tie.

According to the few Oxford and Cambridge graduates on our staff, England has only two universities. Those of us who graduated from civic universities, such as Bristol, Exeter and Southampton were equally disdainful of the *New Polytechnics*. Tony emerged from a *Poly* somewhere in the Midlands and was offered a post at our school chiefly because he was the sole applicant but also because he claimed to share our headmaster's enthusiasm for rugby. He became a fairly competent teacher of mathematics, physics and rugby in spite of his antics much frowned upon by senior staff and, if truth be told, by the more intelligent of his pupils. Tony would prance around in his rolled-up shirt sleeves, perspire profusely and bellow at the pupils to get stuck in. Such a performance and such urgings may have been appropriate on the field but in the opinion of his heads of department there was no place for them in the classroom or the laboratory.

As far as one could tell, Tony had few if any friends on the staff. His principal enemies were the non-smokers who took great exception to the foul-smelling cigarettes of Turkish shag tobacco he rolled in a little machine and smoked in the corner of the common room. He did acquire a small following amongst the younger pupils when he formed a computing club which convened two evenings a week to write programmes and play games on the early machines such as Sinclair's ZX Spectrum, Commodore's Commodore 64 and Acorn's BBC Micro.

When the mathematics department introduced computing science into the curriculum, Tony was asked to teach it. When a computer room was set up for use by the mathematics and science departments, Tony was called upon to maintain it. When computers were introduced into the school office, Tony was asked to train the office staff and to service their machines. Tony became our computer expert. So nobody was surprised when, after five years as a perspiring teacher, he resigned his post to set himself up in business.

'How's his business doing these days?' I asked Cyril as we entered the common room.

'Rather well,' said Cyril. 'He's just formed a second company in point of fact.'

'Was that what you two were talking about in the car park?'

'Yes it was in point of fact,' said Cyril with a *mind your own business look*.

'Want you on his Board of Directors, does he?' I asked wryly.

'In point of fact,' retorted Cyril, catching sight of the slightly sardonic look on my face, 'he's looking for investors.'

'I see. He touched you for a loan.'

'Not at all. He's offered me a short term investment opportunity with a return of 13%.'

'Are you the first one he's approached?'

'In point of fact,' said Cyril, yet again uttering his favourite phrase, 'in point of fact yes, I am.'

'You're what?'' asked Christopher Lovell, our Head of Music, who overheard.

'He's the first one that Tony Simpleton has touched for a loan,' I said.

'An investment,' snapped Cyril. 'He's asked me to invest in his new company.'

'Office Developments (International) Ltd? Is that the company?' Chris asked.

'Yes, I think that's the name,' replied Cyril.

'Then you're not the first. He's already asked me,' said Chris.

'How much does he want you to invest?' asked Cyril, somewhat crestfallen.

'Five thousand pounds. Is that what he asked you for?'

'Yes,' replied Cyril, 'with a return of thirteen percent.'

'If that's 13% per annum,' I said, 'perhaps I should put in £5,000. I'm only getting 7% on my building society savings.' In hindsight, what I should have said was *Thirteen percent sounds too good to be true; so what's the catch*? but I fell victim to the cardinal sins of envy and greed. Pride and wrath were to follow later.

FACTS AND FANTASIES – Volume 1

1. The lawn

This story is a fiction based upon facts personally reported to me and upon events I experienced firsthand. For instance, I knew a chemist, who left a major chemical company, solved a pollution problem, published a book of walks to unusual places, brewed his own wine and who, inspired by the fall of a cast iron gutter that might have killed his son, made his fortune in PVC guttering and downpipes.

2. The axeman cometh

On the 12th of December 1966, Frank Mitchell absconded from Her Majesty's prison high on Dartmoor in the English county of Devon. The following story is true and as accurate as my memory permits. I have not changed the names of the people involved, so I apologise in advance to those (living or dead) mentioned herein who might feel that I have portrayed them in a worse light than I portrayed myself.

3. A tick in a Box

A Canadian source defines bureaucracy as a hierarchy of authority and a system of rules, regulations and record keeping characterized by division of labour and specialization of functions. A British source defines bureaucracy as an excessively complicated administrative procedure. After reading this story, the reader will, I trust, take more care than I did when completing any official form but heed the words of Robert Frost, "If we couldn't laugh, we would all go insane."

4. The journey of a canvas bag

Air is a liquid at minus 200 degrees centigrade. In their research at Bristol University, chemistry students often needed liquid air for their experiments. They kept the liquid in open-necked vacuum flasks to slow its evaporation. This story is based upon an incident that actually took place on a train travelling from Bristol to Southampton around 1958-59. Apart from Bob, all the characters are figments of my imagination. Two of the characters appear in the first story in volume 2 of my collected short stories.

* * * * *

FACTS AND FANTASIES – Volume 3

1. Deception and a deadly switch

The truth underlying this story is the foolish unsecured loans that two colleagues and I made to a former colleague and his brother in 1991. The name of the school, the names of the two companies and the names of the characters, apart from my own, are fictitious. I definitely lost money. I believe I was deceived. I think it best not to comment further.

2. A gorilla in the cupboard

This story concerns a real event I witnessed and a likely consequence I imagined. I have not named the school where this occurred or used the real names of the teachers and pupil concerned in order, hopefully, to avoid costly legal actions. To any former colleagues who were also witness to the event and who might think themselves unfavourably portrayed in my story, may I assert that the names and characters are the product of my imagination and any resemblance to actual persons, living or dead, is entirely coincidental.

3. Water of life

The Bristol-Bordeaux family-to-family exchange began in 1947 with one teacher and twenty-seven pupils from Fairfield Grammar School. The scheme rapidly expanded. In the Easter of 1951, more schools – my own included – were involved and more than one hundred pupils took part - myself included – even though I was no longer studying French. In April 2007, the exchange scheme celebrated its 60th year jubilee.

4. What the eye does not see

My wife and I once owned some timeshare at Castillo Beach Club, a resort on the lower slope of a hill overlooking Caleta de Fuste on Fuerteventura in the Canary Islands. The reception, bar and restaurant were in the main area known as Lake. The other area, known as Moon, was on the other side of the Calle de Virgen de Guadalupe. There are still squirrels on Chipmunk Hill. The supermarket (El Supermercado) and restaurant (El Papagayo) may still operate. I am not sure. The characters and events in this story are pure fantasy but the settings are real enough.

FACTS AND FANTASIES – Volume 4

1. The apple cart

The small retailer has not yet been entirely driven to the wall by the supermarket chain. Some have survived as street traders in open markets which have become popular tourist attractions, e.g. Petticoat Lane in London and Albert Cuypstraat in Amsterdam. In our house here in Canada we still have knick-knacks from flea markets as far afield as the Canary Islands, France and Mexico. This story was conceived as a small tribute to stall owners we encountered around the world. As my research and writing proceeded, it became a tribute to my Canadian friends and SEARIC - their charitable Society for the Education and Assistance of Rural Indian Children.

2. Across a crowded room

On the 6th of August 2010, on the cruise liner Celebrity Constellation, Maureen and I celebrated our Golden Wedding Anniversary. This is the story of how I met my wife. Some of my scientific friends suggest we travel through life encountering people haphazardly as particles collide according to Einstein's mathematical theory of random walk. Maureen and I met by chance they say. Some of my non-scientific friends suggest otherwise. It was kismet they say. Whatever the case, of one thing I can be absolutely sure, I am glad we met.

3. The disappearing chemistry teacher

The central incident in this story occurred in 1960 during my first year of full-time teaching and is described as accurately as my memory will allow. I have given fictitious names to the school and the people involved just in case the long arm of the law could stretch 50 years back in time and instigate prosecutions under the 1974 Health and Safety at Work Act.

4. An alarming business

This story is set in Broadstone, Dorset, where I lived and worked from the Easter of 1971 until I moved to Canada in December 2000. The characters and their goings-on are figments of my imagination but inspired by certain events in which I was involved and by some people whom I held in high regard and about whom I should not, nay would not intentionally write a libellous word.

www.ingramcontent.com/pod-product-compliance
Lightning Source LLC
Chambersburg PA
CBHW070455130626
46555CB00003B/1008